# eleven
# hours

Also by Pamela Erens

*The Virgins*
*The Understory*

# eleven hours

## Pamela Erens

Atlantic Books
London

First published in 2016 in the United States of America by Tin House
Books. First published in hardback and e-book in Great Britain in 2016
by Atlantic Books, an imprint of Atlantic Books Ltd.

This edition published in 2017 by Atlantic Books.

1 2 3 4 5 6 7 8 9

A CIP catalogue record for this book is available from the British Library.

E-book ISBN: 9781782399803

Paperback ISBN: 9781782399810

Printed and bound in Great Britain by Clays Ltd, St Ives plc

Atlantic Books
An Imprint of Atlantic Books Ltd
Ormond House
26–27 Boswell Street
London
WC1N 3JZ

www.atlantic-books.co.uk

*For the billions of women who have been through it,*
*one way or another.*

NO, THE GIRL says, she will not wear the fetal monitoring belt. Her birth plan says no to fetal monitoring.

These girls with their birth plans, thinks Franckline, as if much of anything about a birth can be planned. She thinks *girl* although she has read on the intake form that Lore Tannenbaum is thirty-one years old, a year older than Franckline herself. Caucasian, born July something, employed by the New York City Department of Education. Franckline pronounced the girl's name wrong at first, said "Lorie," and the girl corrected her, said there was only one syllable. *Lore.* Why a girl and not a woman? She arrived here all alone shortly before 9:00 AM, lugging her duffel bag, her tall body pitched to one side with the weight, no man with her, no mother, no friend (and yet a ring on the ring finger of her left hand: a silver band). No one at all, which is almost unheard of: even the homeless addicts sometimes have a man or a friend; even the prostitutes have friends who bring them in. But Lore Tannenbaum does not appear to be an addict or a prostitute. She is wearing clean sweatpants and a clean button-down shirt; her walk, once she set down the duffel, was steady, even graceful; and at the desk she produced an insurance card.

The birth plan, emerging from the packed duffel, is several pages long, many sections, the points single-spaced. There is some sort of long prologue. Lore hands it to Franckline already turned to the correct passage on page 2: *I do not wish to wear a fetal monitor.* The monitor will restrict her to the area near the bed and she wants to be able to move about freely.

"And no IV," Lore Tannenbaum adds. They are the same height, the two women: one ample and softly built, the other more slender and taut, and pregnant as well, but not showing yet, not speaking of it—her anxious secret alone.

Well, you see, explains Franckline, the hospital requires fetal monitoring, could get sued for not using the monitor . . . However, she goes through the play-acting of leaving the labor room to consult with the charge nurse, Marina. Marina returns with her, insists absolutely: legalities, state regulations, etc.

"But Dr. Elspeth-Chang . . ."

Dr. Elspeth-Chang was mistaken, says Marina. Most likely the doctor meant to say that Lore did not have to wear the monitoring belt *continuously*. But she has to wear it now, because she has just arrived, and then for at least fifteen minutes on the hour after that. State law.

"But no IV," agrees Franckline, once Marina is gone, resisting the temptation—the responsibility?—to offer the arguments in favor of it: in an emergency, precious time could be wasted inserting the IV; if Lore changes her mind later (perhaps she will ask for an epidural, even though page 3 of her birth plan says *I do not wish to have an epidural*)—if she changes her mind, dehydration may make the IV difficult to insert. Something about Lore—standing eye to eye with her, her hand on her belly, tremblingly upright (unlike most patients, she does not hunch with pain and anxiety)—silences Franckline. For Lore knows these facts already, she can see, has researched them all before producing her multipage, many-bulleted document.

It is twenty minutes into her hospital stay, thinks Lore, and already she is being thwarted, already opposed and harassed, by these people who want pliancy and regularity, want you to do what is easiest for them rather than what is most sensible and natural. They make you sign forms (*I agree to surrender all control and absolve everyone of blame*) before they will even give you a room and the privacy of your pain. She'd known that once she left her apartment she would be putting herself in the hands of strangers, others whose interests might not coincide with her own. But she did not expect to be so immediately brought down and disheartened. The two nurses, both Caribbean and with hair in braids, good cop and bad cop, one (the charge nurse) blunt, unyielding; the other quiet-voiced, smiling, trying to win her over, make her feel already tired, already beaten. She twists at the ring she wears, grown very tight over these last weeks. The charge nurse had scowled, saying Lore really ought to be going to the triage room, she didn't seem so far along. But Dr. Elspeth-Chang, who had listened to Lore on the phone, had called ahead and said Lore should be admitted, and so Lore simply stood and waited for the charge nurse to finish her grumbling.

"Let's get you comfortable," says the quiet-voiced nurse, Franckline—her accent is of the French-speaking islands, Haiti, maybe, or Guadeloupe—as she helps her onto the hospital bed. A cross swings from a chain around her neck. "You're lucky," she told Lore as soon as she was checked in. "It's very slow on the ward this morning. We can give you one of the private rooms—room 7. There's a large window looking out onto Sixth Avenue." On the deep window ledge, set back, is a potted hibiscus, its leaves a delicate pink with a deeper flame at the center. Would Lore like the bed angled this way or this way? the nurse asks. Up a bit or down?

"Down," says Lore.

In the taxi Lore had held her phone in her palm and flipped the cover up and down, up and down. Not calling Diana or Marjorie, who had promised to get her to the hospital when the time came, to stay with her through the entire thing. Her bag had long been packed; it took her only minutes to leave once she decided to go. She flipped up the phone cover, dialed four digits, pressed END. The cab drove too quickly through the streets, the cabbie's radio too loud with some sort of shrill, sinuous music. Lore dialed a different number—her old number, which was Julia and Asa's now—dialed even as she knew she would not let the call ring through. A heat rose in her chest; her finger moved through the familiar sequence. It was shortly after eight. Asa, large and sloppy in the narrow pass-through kitchen, would be eating his cereal standing up; Julia would be still in bed, trying to coax herself out of her morning torpor. Imagine: Asa picking up the phone, inquiring "Hello?"

in his rich voice, and Lore believing that he could hear in her silence the pains moving through her body, could hear it was time.

She did not want him to come. Never, never. But that he should be rising for his day, comfortable, while she would soon be twisting in pain on a hospital bed . . . that Julia should yawn and stretch and doze again . . .

Imagine: Julia in the bedroom, listening, suspecting, knowing that what she'd set in motion had reached its end point in this child.

*There's someone I need you to meet,* she'd said to Lore.

Lore stopped dialing, stared out the window at the streets racing by: people with takeout coffee in gloved hands, murky morning light against the canopies of apartment buildings. Green wreaths with red baubles in storefronts, the holiday coming soon. The radio, last night, had said something about snow. Lore began picking out Diana's number once more. Then, interrupting herself, leaning forward toward the cabbie—it was more like sliding her whole body sideways across the seat and then pitching herself in his direction—she told him to slow down or she would have the baby right there in the back. The taxi slowed for a minute or two, then picked up speed again. The music shrilled and shrilled until Lore said, in a voice not to be argued with, "Turn the damn radio off."

Why should she call Diana, why should Diana or Marjorie come? She did not know either of them that well. Diana, who taught third grade, and Marjorie, one of the kindergarten aides, had swooped in when Lore announced her pregnancy, very late, at twenty-one weeks, when the visible signs became unmistakable and arrangements had to be made for her leave. She had always been cordial with all of her colleagues but close to none. Her life, for years, had been Asa and Julia. Diana and Marjorie: their outrage on her behalf, their advice, their kale, their jargon ("heroic," "survivor"). How Lore paced her apartment after their visits, guiltily stamping out their condescension and their pity.

"Would you like some water?" asks Franckline.

Lore shakes her head. A girl, yes, a girl, thinks Franckline, but there is something elderly about her as well, something weary. Not the usual weariness Franckline sees, that of a woman who has been up all night and is shaky and frightened, perhaps even her second or third time, but something deeper, something etched into the face—into the young skin that is just beginning to get creases around the eyes and lips—something that goes back a long time. A story I will never fully hear, Franckline thinks, even if she offers bits of it to me. For we only have a matter of hours, and it's the body that concerns us here today, what it needs, what it has no choice but to do. Will Lore want to be touched or not touched, will she want kindness or to be ordered about? Will she let me help her or will she turn her face away as she does now? Will she spend all her time turning away?

The line on the monitor jumps and jags, the speaker reveals the rapid *lub-lub-lub* of the baby's heartbeat. How startling it is to Franckline, still, after all this time: these machines at her disposal, machines that listen to the difference between life and death, that measure and probe and drip chemicals, and save, time and again, souls that can so easily flee the body and disperse. She has watched that flight and that dispersal, not here, not in America, never once (the other nurses say she carries luck with her; each of them has seen tragedies), but back in Ayiti. Babies that got wedged crosswise inside the mother, died there kicking against the womb, or were born already too malnourished to survive. The mothers often enough, too, infected or bleeding or too sick to endure a difficult labor. And the wailing of the burials after, families asking what they had done to displease Danto or Papa Ghede, promising penance, promising gifts, that they will never fail the spirits, the *lwa*, again.

(Franckline moves the monitor toward the patient and turns up the sound so she can hear. *Lub-lub-lub-lub-lub*.

The reassuring babble her own child makes as well. A song to which she sings silently in return: *hallelujah*. But there is no smile, no apparent reaction, from Lore. The girl worries the silver ring on her finger.)

The baby's heart beats like the heart of a runner; the baby *is* a runner, crouched on the starting mark, straining, desperate to begin. Lore has heard the sound twice before but this time she is not moved, only frightened for the baby, its heart frantic with the desire to emerge, to be done with this thing, this birth. The first time, Dr. Elspeth-Chang pointed out the heart on the sonogram machine in her office, but Lore could not see it. The sound the doctor told her was the heartbeat was merely static to her; she wondered for a moment if she'd misunderstood. Then the doctor pointed the sonogram probe at the screen—"There, you see? There"—but to Lore it looked like mist. "I don't see it," she repeated, and the doctor pushed the probe again at the screen and indicated with her finger—all smoke. If Asa had been there he would have seen, or would have convinced himself that he saw. Because Asa. If the sky were covered with gray-black clouds, if you could feel the dampness coalesce thickly and the air sweep upward in threatening gusts, he would say there was a little corner of sunlight in the sky over there—the weather was going to turn for the better.

But of course he was not there. Just weeks before, she had sent him away—or, more precisely, sent herself away, not wanting to remain in their apartment, which contained so many false memories. And the idea of something live beating within that smudge, that smoke, all at once unbalanced her. It was real, the child—and she had chosen. Although of course it was not too late to change her mind. She was only seven weeks along, she could still tell the doctor that she wanted an abortion. She could confess that Asa was not really on a work trip at all. But something inside her knit together and settled and she made her decision anew. She reached out and put her hand on Dr. Elspeth-Chang's arm to stop the motion of the wand. "Oh, well," she said. "Maybe next time."

"Hello, hello," says the resident loudly, coming in. Franckline turns the monitor's speaker down; the baby's heart fades into silence.

The resident—he identifies himself as Dr. Merchant—looks no more than Lore's own age, glossy dark hair waved across his crown, a light shadow on his jaw and chin. A handsome man, too handsome, Lore thinks, to be a doctor. This handsomeness makes him look insufficiently competent. Lore cannot think why this strange, energetic doctor has come in, and then she recalls what the job of the resident is—to examine you. He is standing at the bottom of the bed, looking over at Lore, the hillocks of her breasts and belly, from the vantage point of her feet. For the first time she feels self-conscious in her hospital gown; she tugs at it to close it over her chest.

Dr. Merchant glances at the chart Franckline hands him. "You work for the Department of Education, huh?" he asks. "You're a speech therapist? How do you like that?" He pulls on his surgical gloves.

"When was your last contraction?" he asks. Franckline helps Lore's feet into the stirrups.

Not since leaving her apartment, she begins; she thinks the movement of the cab put the baby into a kind of— "Okay, relax," the doctor says. "Now—" and he puts his fingers inside her. There is a strong, dull pain, a pain that makes her throat fill up. She concentrates on staying still and breathing in and out— must he stay there so long?—and on a beige square inside her head that seems the best equivalent of nowhere that she can come up with. The doctor removes his fingers and wipes them briskly on a towel.

"Now what were you saying?"

Not since her apartment, she explains, gratefully accepting the damp washcloth Franckline hands her, patting at her sweaty forehead and nose and neck. She left the house before eight. What time is it now?

"Just after nine," the doctor tells her.

"They were coming every four minutes before I left."

She had been determined not to get to the hospital too early. Her books said, her childbirth instructor said, that the earlier you got to the hospital the more chance there was that the doctors would come up with something to speed you up or slow you down, or run tests on you "just in case," or hook you up to some machine or other—the more likely you were to end up with a C-section or at the very least an episiotomy. There were statistics to prove all this. *Try to wait until six or seven centimeters,* her childbirth instructor had said, but who knew when that was? *You'll have a pretty good idea,* said the instructor. *The contractions will be every four to five minutes and the quality of the pain changes. It becomes more intimate, more intense.*

Well, in her apartment the pains, which had woken her at about 3:00 AM, were fierce enough to send Lore crouched on all fours clutching the pipes under the bathroom sink, pulling hard against them. You were supposed to relax and breathe, but she soon discovered it felt much better to pull hard at the pipes and curse loudly. The pains were intense, yes—but had she failed to let them become "intimate" enough? At six she called work and told them her labor had started. At seven thirty she got in touch with Dr. Elspeth-Chang's answering service. When the doctor called back, fifteen minutes later, she had Lore hold the phone while she went through a contraction and told her, yes, it's time to go in, I'll call ahead.

Cursing under the pipes: *Motherfucker cocksucking mother-shitting . . .*

"You seem to be taking a bit of a break," says the doctor. "In any case, you're at three centimeters. Fifty percent effaced, minus-two station."

Three centimeters? Three centimeters? The pipes under the sink and Dr. Elspeth-Chang calling ahead and she is at three centimeters?

"Your water hasn't broken yet, so it's probably going to be a while. You might want to go home. Do you live far?"

"Yes," says Lore. Oh, yes, she lives far. She had to go far to be able to afford no roommates, a place where she and the baby-to-be could be alone. She can't bear the thought of going all the way back to Jackson Heights and then having to return again, not to mention the expense of two more taxi rides. "Like I said, they were coming every four minutes before I left. Maybe every three."

The doctor pauses. "All right." He looks at Franckline, and they exchange a glance—the girl is alone, she's at forty weeks, it's not busy this morning. "Let's see what happens over the next hour or so. We'll take good care of you," he assures Lore. He waits for a returning smile, but she does not oblige.

"Would you like another damp cloth?" asks Franckline, when the doctor has gone out. For a cold sweat is upon Lore again. Lore nods. "Don't pay too much attention to the numbers," the nurse tells her. "You can spend six hours getting to three centimeters and then go from there to ten in forty-five minutes. It doesn't mean that much."

"Why do they check, then?"

Franckline removes the chilly cloth. "Because we all like to measure things," she says. She'll call Dr. Elspeth-Chang and give her the news. In the meantime, Lore should rest; she'll be glad for it later.

But just as she says this Lore feels a contraction coming at last, starting somewhere in her back and moving layer by layer toward the deepest, most interior part of her pelvis, then seeming to radiate back out from there, pushing and spreading as if to press out of her skin. Franckline has been sitting next to the bed but now stands up. There's no time for Lore to get into a more comfortable position. On her back, as she is now, she is trapped and helpless, unable to meet the hurt with anything of her own. Her cervix is the pit of a fruit—apricot, peach—that is being pried apart to release something new: a juice or a green shoot. Her face twists and she draws up her knees and pushes down as if she were already pushing the baby out, but this is a mistake, the pit is not ready to come open and it resists her, spraying her with pain. Lore rolls from side to side on the bed, calling out, "Oh, no! Oh, no!" She hears herself, and is ashamed of this voice, of the panic in it. But: *Oh, no! Oh, no!* it says, and *Oh, no!* again, and then, finally, she is able to tell her voice to stop, to shut up, and she merely sways, clenching her jaw as the pain gradually diminishes and seeps back out of her body. Diana, she thinks. Ma. Ma! But her mother, the last time she saw her, was a gray face on a cot in the living room, murmuring, *Listen, you'll get money from the policy I paid into, you'll be able to move someplace else if you want, you'll get on with your life . . .*

"That was a good long one," Franckline tells her. "Forty seconds."

Lore turns her head away in self-reproach. "I didn't . . . I wasn't ready."

"It's all right. There are some things we can do to make the next one easier. For starters, let's get you off your back."

"Don't tell me to do the breathing," Lore warns. "I'm sick of hearing about the breathing."

"I'm not saying anything about any breathing."

Lore shifts to her side and lets Franckline gently help her to a seated position. It is then that Franckline notices how tightly Lore's ring pinches her.

"Your finger," she says, pointing her chin in the direction of Lore's left hand.

Lore spreads it in front of her eyes—what of it?

"It's swollen. You should have that ring off. The finger isn't getting the proper circulation."

Lore shrugs.

"They have a tool here that can cut it. I'll call for someone."

"No," says Lore. And though she says it quietly, there is finality in it. Franckline has rarely heard such a "no" from a woman. Where did Lore learn to say hers? What makes her believe it will be honored?

Franckline reaches for Lore's hand—Lore does not protest this action—and gazes down at the palm. There is flesh bunched below the wide silver band on the fourth finger, like a thick putty squeezing out. The ring, though substantial, is swallowed up by the large hand. It is engraved with some abstract pattern of repeating and interlocking L shapes. The finger above the ring is paler than the other fingers, with a blueish tinge. Franckline should tell Lore in no uncertain terms, in her practiced nurse's voice, that the ring must be cut, that she could lose the finger. Franckline should use a word like *necrotize*, a word that makes young women pale and listen. But Lore would simply repeat "no." Franckline can feel it up and down her nerves. Nevertheless it would be unprofessional, irresponsible, not to press the matter. Her responsibility just now is to the finger, not to Lore. That is, to Lore's body and not to whatever thoughts cause Lore to frown and to so firmly refuse.

"Yes," Franckline says. "You will lose the finger."

The girl laughs. It is sudden and full of mirth. Franckline sees that the girl's face can be pretty, under the right kind of expression. Until now it has been merely a pale, moon-shaped, not especially distinctive face. Light-brown irises and shoulder-length hair of an indeterminate brown color. A face you don't focus on in a crowd, that your eyes slide away from on the subway. Not like Franckline's own (why deny it?), long and sculpted with deep-set eyes and, Bernard says, the elegant neck of a movie star. The girl is laughing and Franckline can see that she has a pretty self as well, a self more delicate and tender that contradicts her heavy, doleful energy. It is a hidden self, though, wary and watching.

"I'm not going to lose a finger," Lore says delightedly.

"You could. Yes, you could."

"No, I won't."

Let the girl laugh. But it will be Franckline's fault, in the end, if anything happens. Stiffly, she says, "We will check on it later. To make sure it doesn't get any worse. Look, you can take the monitor off now if you like."

"It's coming again," Lore says, as soon as Franckline is done removing the belt and placing it near the monitor screen. "I want to get onto my hands and knees."

Franckline tips Lore forward as if she were a sort of rocking horse, and helps her untuck her legs from beneath her.

"Thank you," breathes the girl. So she has manners, at least.

This time, as the contraction mounts, she does not cry out, but her face is tense and grim. In fighting back her cries of fear she is fighting her body, too, and Franckline can feel the inner muscles clenching against the descending head, rendering the long moment of suffering unproductive. She does not touch the girl; she can feel as clearly as she feels the constriction of the muscles that the girl does not want to be touched. How insistent she is, how rigid. How pointless it is to fight the body and the pain it sends, stretching and widening one to make new life, demanding that the self fall back and make space. Make space! Pointless to fight it. Yet nearly all of them do, crying, screaming, praying, begging Franckline to make it stop, to reel back the forces of being. She has known that since she was a child. She was no more than six years old; every time there was a birth in her village she would run, more than a mile if necessary, to be there. Nearly faint with excitement and anticipation: would the woman bleed a lot, develop a fever, would she scream loudly or just whimper, would she live, would the baby live? She was compelled to see what might happen. The deep groans of the squatting woman, the way her sisters and aunties and cousins would cluster around her, gripping her arms and steadying her hips, running with sweat all of them, the parched lips and the low humming songs; it was like the races the older boys and young men sometimes ran against each other, the strain of bodies pushed to their limits, the pain, the exhaustion, the glory in the finish, but better because more violent: the head crowning at the end, the blood mixed with the sparse hair, the last push and the last groan, the woman released at last, muttering, weeping, cradled by the arms of the sisters and aunties and cousins.

And no one prevented her from watching. She saw everything. Somehow the others knew not to shoo her from the door. She learned to bring tea leaves and massage the scalp of a woman in the early stages of labor. They called her Ti Matrone, the little midwife. Over time she absorbed the practicalities: when to make the woman walk, when to make her drink, when to wait. By the time she was eleven or twelve she knew how to turn a breech baby, apply herb compresses for heavy bleeding, make a woman expel a baby that had died. The villagers said she had the gift, she was what they called *pon*, or bridge, could bring life safely from there to here, from the womb to the world. Of course there were times when the babies died. The mothers too. But mostly Erzulie Mapiangue favored Franckline when she attended at a birth, and protected the laboring mother. Back then others' pain did not touch her, had nothing to do with her; not until after her own child—then.

The girl, Lore, beyond the contraction again, lowers herself onto her side and lies there, hot misery radiating from her skin. "I thought I would be better at this," she says.

Franckline pulls a chair up close. "Let me ask you. You can yell, can't you?"

The girl is silent.

"Here is what you do. You are right, you can forget that deep-breathing nonsense. Nobody can breathe through those pains. When the next one comes, I want you to take one big breath and then yell, but very slowly, you understand? Not with your mouth but from the back of your throat, deep." Franckline demonstrates, rumbling her voice up in a quiet groan. "But louder.

You yell in slow motion, making it last as long as you can. Okay? We'll practice when you're ready."

"I'm ready now."

"Good."

"Help me onto my hands and knees."

"Now," says Franckline, when Lore is in place. "Draw in a lot of air—down into your belly—and yell it back out. Slowly."

"UUUUUHHHHHHHH."

I can open this girl, Franckline thinks. She will open. "Not bad, but you can do better than that."

"UUUUUHHHHHHAAAAAAAAAKKKKK."

"Don't close up the throat."

"UUUUUUUUHHHHHHHHHHHHHHAAAAAAAAA."

"That's better. That's better. You do that when the next one comes."

"Help me down," says Lore. She rests, and then wakes with a startle. She can tell that she's slept no more than a minute. Franckline is still beside her as before, and she can just remember the thought, or rather the image, right before she dropped. She was dialing a phone in a taxi, trying to push swollen fingers at the small keys. Then she dropped. And in that short minute she went somewhere else, into an apartment she has never been in, where a woman with snow-white hair was serving her beautiful small cakes on a platter.

The platter, silver, gleamed brightly. Lore dithered over which cake to take first—they were all so appealing—and then, before she could put her fingers around one, someone shrieked loudly, as if to shoo her away.

She hears it again now—the shriek. It was the noise that woke her. It is a woman somewhere down the hall, and Lore blames her for taking away the platter of cakes. It was wonderful to have been there, in that severely well-appointed room, attempting to choose something sweet. Although now that she is awake she does not like the thought of food at all. The apartment had something in it of Asa's parents' apartment, of Helen Fox's impeccably ordered library. The woman shrieks again. In childbirth class Lore and her classmates saw movies of women who did not scream and did not panic, but bore their pain with athletic grimaces. She had been in a temper every Wednesday at six thirty in the evening, in the big room above a city gym, tired from the day spent coaxing second and third graders to pick up M&Ms by sucking on a straw. As she walked from the subway, her hips twinged at each step. Sometimes, through one hip, there shot a bolt of pain so strong that she had to stop while other people bumped her and cursed. It felt as if the hip was coming unhinged from the leg, as if it was going to snap out at some strange angle like a puppet's. These twinges, these bolts, had come on around the seventh month. All sorts of things had happened at the seventh month. Eating anything spicy made her ill for days. She could not tolerate milk. She had gas and hiccups.

She knew that there were other women in the childbirth group who came straight from work, without even a break for dinner, in their maternity blazers and heels that pinched their swollen feet, but even so, even though she had time to go home from P.S. 30 and drink a little tea and have a little meal, she was in a temper every Wednesday and could not bring herself to like the class. The plumpish instructor, her own children grown and gone, was a nice woman, well-meaning, yet Lore was irritated by every word she spoke. Why? Why should she dislike Betsy, the instructor, or Melissa and John from 74th Street or Catherine and Peter from Summit, New Jersey? Was it because, as her mother would have put it, they looked like money? Why did Jane and Cecily's plans to have Cecily birth the baby in their feng-shui'd bathroom cause Lore to smile with condescension? For a short time (Diana's influence), she herself had flirted with using the bathtub. Perhaps that was what it was— these other women, these *couples*, still believed in what they could imagine, still enjoyed building up in their minds their perfect homes, their perfect births.

Whereas she, the one partnerless woman, the one who always had to team up with the instructor for the exercises, stood precisely for the fact that things did not turn out as you had planned. Betsy massaged Lore's back, showing the muscle groups that John and Peter and Jane should press on during the labor, to release tension. She held Lore's hand, to demonstrate the importance of loving touch.

When she got home from class, there would be another message from Asa on her answering machine. Lore thinks it must have been Marjorie who got in touch with him. A couple of times Marjorie had asked her nervously whether she'd spoken to Asa, and didn't she think he had the right to know about the baby? No matter what had happened? And mightn't being in touch help, you know, financially?

Diana overheard and scolded Marjorie terribly. Asa had slept with *Lore's best friend*, she reminded her. And Lore didn't need some asshole's help: she had a good job and good benefits, she would manage on her own. Very sure of Lore, very cavalier about Lore's finances, was Diana.

The shrieking woman has fallen silent. Maybe she is all right. Maybe the baby has emerged and it is all over for her. Maybe they gave her an injection that took away the pain.

"Would you like some water?" asks Franckline.

"Yes, please."

Franckline brings her a paper cup from the sink, and when Lore is done with it offers more. After three cupfuls Lore sinks back onto the bed feeling much better, as if her veins and tendons had needed watering. She sighs. It is not so bad to lie here between pains, waiting, daydreaming. She likes the silence, and she likes Franckline for preserving it. A bolt of sun pierces the big window, dashing a stripe onto her blue hospital gown and warming her face. Soon she will sit in the rocking chair on deposit at Babies 'R Us (she would not take it home with her, nor has she stenciled the living room, nor put together the crib: it is not good to tempt fate)—soon she will sit in such an offering of winter sun, a single ray warming the baby and the breast at which it suckles, and they will rock and rock in a shaft of time that has stilled just for them. While the baby sleeps Lore will cook green things in a big skillet, and water the plants: the geranium and the coleus and, in honor of her mother, the Starfighter lilies tended from the bulb all winter. Her mother had labored patiently over her lilies in the rocky little yard of their house in Hobbes Corners. Lilies her favorite, but there were also cosmos and phlox, tulips and roses. At night, moonlight drinkers tossed empty bottles onto their lawn.

Then her mother got sick. Multiple myeloma. Lore's father, gone long before this: blurred images of a man in a cream-colored sweater with leather patches on the elbow. As a child, Lore liked to run her finger across the smoothness of those patches onto the coarse hairiness of the knit, shivering at the transition. The wearer of this garment disappeared by the time she was four. Apparently the three of them had once lived in a small Greenwich Village apartment, a place Lore did not remember at all. A law school student, her mother claimed. She did not say where they had met, or how; in fact she spoke of him only very rarely in a tone meant to dissuade questions. But apparently his parents, Jewish, had disapproved of her, a Catholic girl with only a tenth-grade education. When the marriage, never stable, disintegrated, Lore and her mother had gone to live with Aunt Janine in Lockport, New York. Lore remembers the arguments between the two sisters, Aunt Janine shouting and her mother hissing quietly in response, the separate stashes of flatware and glasses, her mother's tears at night in the room that they shared and that even at four years old Lore knew Aunt Janine begrudged them (it was her son Sam's room—Sam who now had to double up with his older brother). At some point before grade school they moved forty miles or so to Hobbes Corners, and then

Lore did not have an aunt anymore. There were grand-
parents—Lore remembers occasional visits, both older
people chain-smoking—but later, somehow, there
were not. For a couple of years, Christmas presents still
arrived from them: gifts that broke easily or seemed
designed for a child younger than herself.

Junior year of high school: coming home to find
her mother lying on the couch, having left work early
and too tired to lift the remote to turn off a program
in which two middle-aged men were arguing about
Central Europe. Her eyes were hidden behind an
unhealthy film. Days of missed work, Lore on the
phone with her mother's longtime boss begging him
not to fire her, promising that they were seeing doctors, getting tests, figuring out what the matter was.
Senior year: driving to chemo appointments, trying to
cook food her mother would find palatable, managing the paperwork to get her her disability payments.
Her mother insisting that Lore apply to college, Lore
refusing. Then her mother back at work at the taxi
dispatcher's and Lore starting at Stuyvesant College,
fifteen miles away. The relapse, more chemo, more
treatment, more pain, more bureaucracy. Lore got her
classwork done and managed to stay in school, but she
never found the time to make friends, and finally it
was as if she'd lost the knack of it. Four years of her

mother's illness contracted around her and squeezed her into a different shape, so that she became detached and careful, a provisional sort of person, someone who did not believe in the day after next. Then her mother was truly better, but Lore stayed close by and kept her heart free, afraid to be spirited away by some love affair or ambitious impulse—because What If?

It is coming again. The pain is signaling from a distance, beginning to press her. Lore struggles up to her hands and knees, Franckline steadying her as she rises ponderously above her own weight. "Now yell," says Franckline. Lore takes a deep breath and holds her mouth open in a large O, to give the sound the biggest possible exit. The breath, the O, causes words to appear in her mind, and the words are *Fuck you.* Fuck who? It doesn't matter. She breathes air deep into her belly, makes an O, and her mind agrees: *Fuck you.* She propels from her mouth a great moan that grows louder as the pain builds. When she runs out of moan she inhales again and pushes out a new voice stronger than before. *Fuck you and you and you.* Fuck you, fuck everyone. Fuck you all, fuck off, you millionfold little fuckers. The sound she is making is so loud that it stops up her ears. The moan and the pain run side by side, both tenacious, both insistent, but finally the pain begins to drop off and Lore lets the moan slacken a bit, too: a jog now, a trot, a walk, and then both sound and pain come to a stop.

A moment passes. Then another. Lore lifts her head. Franckline has stepped aside and is looking at her with a smile, impressed. Their eyes meet. Franckline starts to laugh heartily, and Lore laughs too.

The monitoring belt has gone on and off, on and off. It is past noon. Franckline spends time in other rooms and takes her lunch, leftovers from the pork dish Bernard made last night. He is not a man to avoid the kitchen. He gets home earlier in the evening than she does, and he likes to have it smelling of meat and vegetables by the time she arrives.

Franckline nibbles at her dish. Every bite carries a taste of rancid oil, although she knows everything in their house is fresh. It's her, her changed body chemistry. It is time to tell Bernard about the baby. This girl in room 7, so solitary, so wary, seems a sort of warning. Franckline should not become like that, a person too shut up in herself, too frightened and proud to share her pain. There is a side of her, she knows, that gravitates in that direction, toward that pride, that aloneness. At first she had told herself she would speak to Bernard at the end of the first trimester, when the earliest risks would be over; then she wanted one more week to be sure, and now two more than that have gone by. It is wrong to keep Bernard out. But it is so terrible to speak. It is in the later weeks that the worst dangers will come: her water breaking too early, pre-term labor, deformity leading to death in the womb. If she tells Bernard about the child, only to lose it, she will feel as if she has once again stolen from him the life that he should be having with her, and that he could be having with someone else. Does he sometimes regret—in a pause at his office, or while speaking to his mother on the phone—approaching a skinny and scared girl of eighteen on the steps of the Port-au-Prince Cathedral, standing between her and a different end to her story?

Just one more week, perhaps?

She packs up the rest of her lunch—that is, nearly all of it—and places the container with her name on it back in the nurses' refrigerator. A thread of melody passes through her mind. She searches for its origin and locates it. Something one of her nieces, Karen, warbled last weekend, while Franckline and Bernard were at his older sister's apartment. Karen, a shy, serious five-year-old, had gone away from the others to play with a doll. The little children usually sang jingles from commercials, the older ones whatever was on MTV. Karen sang a tune that had the progressions and undulations of the Caribbean in it. It was not a contemporary song but something older, something no one person had written. Who had sung it to her; where had she found it? Karen's three older brothers and sisters lounged and roughhoused in the small rooms. Their mother swatted at them good-naturedly as they passed. Franckline stood rooted, deeply startled. It was a tune she had never heard before and one she was convinced she knew.

She would like the surprise of children, the way they bring pieces of the outer world back to you, pieces of the past, present, and future. The way they are always in a place where you cannot quite meet them.

She wipes the table with a napkin and looks at her watch. There are still fifteen minutes left on her break but she decides to return directly to Lore's room. She is uneasy about letting the girl out of her sight for too long.

Marina catches her on her way back, beckons for Franckline to come over. "The program is locking me out again. Franckline, I swear . . ."

Franckline looks from the screen to the keyboard and taps a few keys. Nothing happens, so she goes into Systems and monkeys around in there. The hospital introduced a new computer system last month and there are still a lot of glitches. Franckline doesn't know that much more about computers than the other nurses, but she's less afraid of doing the wrong thing.

Some of her colleagues seem to think that if they press the wrong combination of keys they'll make the whole system go down, or erase an entire week's scheduling.

In a few minutes Franckline has Marina back on the page she needs, a requisition for upgraded newborn scales.

"I don't know how you figure it out," Marina says, a bit grudgingly.

"I keep telling you, you don't have to figure it. Just mess with it. There's always a way to undo what you've done."

The nurse in room 7 puts down the magazine she's been reading and reports, before going out, that it's been twelve minutes since Lore's last contraction. Lore lies in her bed, unspeaking but restless. She laboriously shifts position and then, a few moments later, shifts again. She breathes heavily. She says she wishes things would keep going.

"Yes, yes," says Franckline, soothingly. What more can she say? She learned long ago never to make promises to a woman in labor. Fast labors slow down, slow labors become fast. Anything can happen, and often does. Women who say they will never accept an epidural beg for the epidural, beg to be knocked out entirely. Babies twisted up in the umbilical cord, starved of oxygen for a little too long. Birthmarks obliterating a child's face, absent fingers or toes. Fifty-hour labors, a mother suffering a heart attack while pushing (that one was only thirty-two years old, grossly overweight, yes, but seemingly hale, with an energetic, generous laugh; they saved her, but it was touch and go). And of course there was Franckline's own child, three days old (he would never be more than three days old), who never once cried, but a few times lifted a weak half fist to punch the sky.

"Yes, yes"—such a weak phrase. It needles her briefly with shame. *Yes, yes* and *no, no*: these were the only two sentences she could bring out of herself when she first came to the States. I agree, I don't agree. I accept, I reject. The two elemental positions, when everything else has been taken away. Those first weeks in New York, scared out of her ability to recollect anything in the Kreyol-English textbook Bernard had made her study.

"Have you a book, or some music?" she asks Lore. Lore shakes her head and twists at that worrisome ring. Well, then, can she turn on the TV? Another no. Franckline feels a flickering of exasperation. Why is there so much No in this girl? Why does she seem to take a grim pleasure in having nothing, no one, in refusing distraction or comfort?

Franckline takes Lore's chart from the pouch beside the door and peruses it again. She removes Lore's birth plan and sits down with it at the computer desk. She scanned it first thing when Lore arrived but has yet to read it point by point. The date on it is about six weeks ago, October 27, 2004. Lore has organized the plan under different headings: there are REQUESTS; IN-TERVENTIONS; IN THE EVENT OF A C-SECTION; BABY CARE IMMEDIATELY AFTER BIRTH; IN THE EVENT THAT THE BABY IS ILL OR HANDICAPPED; IN THE EVENT THAT THE BABY DIES.

> IN THE EVENT THAT THE BABY DIES, I seek the following:
>
> - *to be able to see and hold the baby for as long as I wish*
> - *not to be given tranquilizers or drugs that blunt feeling*
> - *to arrange the funeral myself*

Lore stares up at the ceiling, as if searching there for the baby who may or may not arrive, who will probably live but also might conceivably die. Franckline silently offers her admiration. Most birth plans specify that the patient wants a natural childbirth or hot compresses to reduce the chance of an episiotomy, wants to room in with the baby and so forth. But the babies in these plans are never going to have deformed hearts or damaged brains. They are always going to be born with the right number of limbs; they are always going to survive.

There is another form, a health proxy, tucked behind the birth plan. *I, Lore Tannenbaum of New York, New York, being of sound mind . . . these instructions apply if I am permanently unconscious, or conscious but have irreversible brain damage . . . I do not want mechanical respiration . . . I do not want tube feeding . . . Witnessed by Diana Massie, residing at 501 Manhattan Ave., NY, NY . . .* Franckline flips back a few pages. Lore requests no Demerol. No Pitocin. No epidural. No supplementary bottles. No enema. No shaving.

No, no, and again no.

"I went over all of that with Dr. Elspeth-Chang," says Lore.

"Yes," says Franckline. She returns the plan to its folder. "Let's take a walk," she announces. "It might get you going again." This may be true but will more likely simply serve as a distraction for Lore. She adds: "Having a child is usually just a long patience."

How supple her speech is now! How she surprises herself at times! She is proud of her English; after eleven years it is almost flawless. After that first fright she took to it quickly, making her new neighbors, the ones of long residence, talk with her, correct her. Bernard said: *You see, I told you. You have brains, quickness. You've got to study and get into school. Here you could become a nurse.*

She stands close while Lore pushes herself off the bed, ready to lend a hand, but Lore is steady on her feet. The hallway is more brightly lit than the labor room, although the tan-yellow linoleum floor has a sickly hue. Lore moves slowly now. They pass an empty room, and then another to which Marina assigned a fifteen-year-old shortly before Lore arrived. Often Franckline gets the teenagers, because Marina knows she has the patience for them, won't lecture them when they cry that pushing is "too hard" or eat Ring Dings and drop the wrappers on the floor. Franckline gets many of the difficult cases: she is seen as good with the obstreperous, the addled, the distraught. But this girl and her mother spoke mostly Spanish, so Marina gave the room to Alta. Franckline can hear the mother speaking to her daughter in a low, rapid voice, as if she has something urgent to impart before the baby's arrival. A whiff of fast-food burger wafts out of the open door, making Franckline queasy. Surely the girl can't be eating one.

They walk. Lore stops for a moment to adjust her gown, which has gotten caught up between her legs. All day the laboring and their caretakers trickle in and filter out and are replaced by different girls, women, husbands, mothers, sisters, friends. After today, Franckline will never again see this young woman with limp, mussed hair who has just exited room 11, Elmo slippers on her feet, heading toward the nurses' station; or the girl, ten or twelve years old, about to become somebody's older sister or cousin, who is repeatedly filling a conical cup at the water cooler and dumping the water back down the drain. Franckline feels a helpless, pulsing goodwill toward them all, tiny fragments of the great whole busy life of the universe that God in His goodness allows to unfold in her vision.

Touching her cross, she passes the mussed-hair woman, the girl, and they dissolve back into the mystery of who they are and where they soon will be going. Outside a closed room sits a man wearing a Mets cap, his hands folded in his lap. Hispanic, probably Dominican, Franckline thinks, in his midtwenties or so. Franckline greets him and the man tips up his chin in acknowledgment. A muffled cry arises from within the room, and then, right afterward, the patter of women speaking, comforting. The man stares at his palms and hums quietly to himself. Inside is women's work; the place for a man is out here. That has never been Bernard's style. Even that last time, when Franckline was rushed here in premature labor at twenty-two weeks,

Bernard stayed in the room for the whole messy, agonizing thing.

At the double doors, past a smaller nurses' station, a
wall plaque displays an arrow to Pulmonary. The station nurse nods to Franckline and buzzes them through.
The corridor here, though it looks exactly like the one in
Maternity, has its own distinct and different atmosphere
and smell: more vinegar, less sweat. It is emptier, more
disquieting. Lore takes her time. About halfway down
the first long line of doors, a clatter arises, and abruptly
a wheelchair is beside them, with a man in perhaps his
late seventies inside. Small, trim, with yellowed white
hair, he turns to look at Lore with alert eyes. As the chair
moves ahead, pushed by a young, dark-haired nurse, he
twists back to keep her in his sight, and unexpectedly,
Lore breaks into a responsive smile. In a loud voice, the
man says, "You'll be fine, dear."

"Okay," Lore replies. Her smile disappears but she
doesn't seem angry. Her shoulders loosen, her walk becomes more relaxed. The wheelchair reaches another
set of double doors and the nurse pushes through.
Franckline watches as the soles of her waffled sneakers
lift and fall and disappear. Then:

"Oh," Lore says. "Oh, no."

"Right here," Franckline tells her, firmly, and, absurd
as this seems, as appalled as Lore is, she obeys. Right

there, on the old linoleum (she can feel its cracks and bumps etch themselves into the tender skin of her knees), she goes down and she remembers; she opens her mouth and her throat and urges out the great noise that mounts and crests and finally rolls back its force again. The external world disappears; all she hears is her own sound; she is a cave filled with a great echoing voice. When she is done she closes her eyes for a moment, returning to herself. Franckline helps her to her feet. There are two elderly women standing opposite, gazing at her. One, in a hospital gown with a cardigan thrown over it, an arm covered with purple bruises, stares blankly; the other, dressed in slacks and a silky blouse, her still-ample hair puffed around her temples and ears, holding her friend's wrist, wears an expression of distaste.

"She's in labor," Franckline explains, calmly, and this articulation of the obvious makes the disapproving woman's eyes lose their sharpness. She tips her head in acquiescence and turns to her friend. "She's going to have a baby," she says, as if the friend doesn't already understand, and perhaps she doesn't, because she simply licks her lips tremblingly several times.

"Let's go back," says Lore. She feels a strange glee: she has flung her pain into this public space, not caring who observed it, whom she discomfited. This is possible, then; this can be done! But all the same a reflexive sense of embarrassment makes her turn from the two women and pretend she doesn't see them. There is something questioning in the fashionably dressed one's gaze that she doesn't want to encounter. Perhaps she is asking how Lore was able to do it, to release her pain so rudely. In childbirth class Betsy spent a whole day talking about the history of men's handling of women in labor: the withholding of pain relief or dosing patients into oblivion or putting them in restraints. Cutting tools that didn't need to be used, the shaving, the assault of the forceps. This woman is old enough to have experienced some or all of that. In her questioning eyes her story of pain is spilling silently out. But Lore does not want to know that story. There is time, right now, for her own pain only.

Yes, they need to go back. But they will have to cross deserts and seas to return! It took them weeks to gain this distance; Lore is far away from rest.

They turn toward Maternity, and Franckline now allows herself to think of the odd twinge she felt while Lore was down on the floor riding the contraction. She thought it might be a sympathetic effect, the absorption of a neighboring pain into her own body. But it continues as they make their way back. (Edie, a nurse in Pulmonary, smiles at them as she briskly passes.) And now Franckline feels a sharp stab on the left above her groin.

*By week 15 of pregnancy your baby may suck its thumb. Eyes are at the front of the face but are still widely separated.*

She has seen the drawings and the sonograms and the uterine photographs hundreds of times, knows every detail of fingernails, eyelashes, crown-to-rump length. She learned these in nursing school, and she learned them too from the books she bought the last time she was pregnant. For over five years she and Bernard did not conceive, though both believed it would happen eventually, that God would grant it to them at the right time, and then He did. But she lost that pregnancy at twenty-two weeks. First there was backache, then the shock of her water breaking as she sat on the toilet massaging herself against the pain. It took seven hours to deliver the fetus, which had a weak heartbeat and died as soon as the cord was cut. She was told later that the pancreas and liver were underdeveloped, not to mention the lungs; there had been absolutely no chance of survival. The imaging afterward revealed that Franckline possessed a bicornate uterus—a uterus split into two chambers. There was possible cervical insufficiency as well. What will be, will be, Bernard said, and he seemed to mean it, but Franckline covertly visited a *mambo* to propitiate Ki Titha and Erzulie Mapiangue all the same. Six years passed, six years during which she finally put aside the idea of another pregnancy, and now here is a child inside of her again.

The staff here, mostly kind and attentive, has been watching her closely. Young Dr. Roper hooked her up on Tuesday to one of the ultrasound machines and said, yes, the heart is beating, the head and limbs look absolutely normal, terrific, Franckline. They will give her the best possible care, the best that is out there to be had. Some days she is sure this fetus will cleave to her long enough, will insist on being born with a healthy heart and lungs and limbs. Other days she is equally sure she can feel its lack of will in the face of the odds, and she grows despondent. She does not wholly believe Bernard when he says, as he has, over and over, that it does not matter to him, that he does not need a child. He is not truly as American as all that. Or perhaps it is she who cannot be quite so American. Her body once birthed a child, and ever since then it has ached to be a shelter again. *It could be my last chance, yes?* she asked Dr. McKenna, the high-risk specialist. She knew what his answer would be but she wanted to hear his tones, his inflection. Perhaps then she would know how to adjust her expectations up or down the scale of hope. "You never know," he replied. He was a professional; there was no inflection at all. But she knows that with every miscarriage, the likelihood of her ever having a healthy child decreases.

The pregnancy has made her mean, made her small, Franckline thinks. On the subway and in the streets, she looks away from pregnant women—seven, eight, nine months along—so as not to poison them with her envy. The women who come into the labor ward are different; they are in their time of need; they are her charges, her children. But outside, she poisons the air with her resentment. When the subway train lurches forward, bringing her out of her post-work doze, she thinks for a moment that she felt the child move inside her, but of course it's way too early for that. Surely Bernard must guess—her diminished appetite, her reticence in bed. It is not right that she has not told him. The man was fashioned to be a father. Infants fall instantly asleep on his shoulder, older children run to him with a ball or jump rope, knowing he will agree to play. He has prospects at work and will provide more and more for the household as he advances. But what is the point of more money if they do not have a family? What then had they come here for?

Dr. Roper told her, "Beautiful—a beautiful, normal baby, Franckline." That was only days ago. But now the stabbing pain near the ovaries, shooting into the womb.

When they return to the birthing room, Franckline tells Lore she must go to the restroom, she will be right back. "Going to use the restroom," she repeats to Marina, who gestures to Carol to replace her in room 7. Franckline uses the bathroom farthest from the nurses' station, because if she finds what she fears, she may cry out. She closes the stall door and pulls down her scrubs, her underpants. She already pictures the star-shaped print of blood on the cotton panel. But there is nothing there. She sits, panting, on the toilet, releases a trickle of urine that makes her feel she has gotten rid of some bad news. Her stomach unclenches. But this is just one moment of reassurance, and there are so many more minutes—hundreds of thousands of minutes—to get through before the baby can be born. May 31—that is the date, if the baby lives. Franckline stands, flushes the toilet, washes her hands at the sink.

The baby that never cried, that raised its fist to the sky—it scraped her out, made her womb unfit to carry any more children. That baby that was fashioned so easily, out of the one time she let Maarten stay inside her. He had insisted that pulling out reduced his seed, would shrivel him over time like a curse from Ki Titha. She was only sixteen but she knew better. She heard a great deal from the laboring women she helped along. And nearly everyone knew that if the man didn't pull out you might get SIDA. But she let him stay that one time. Fatigue from fighting him, maybe. Maybe the sense of loneliness when the man's body withdrew so quickly, and you felt the cold between your legs and the abrupt sense of separateness again.

She was lucky her mother and father did not beat her or force her to become Maarten's woman when she swelled up with his child. Most daughters would have suffered that. Maarten, with his unblemished skin, his slim hips, his pretty singing voice. She hadn't been fooled for a moment by his talk of love, of promising to care for her always; she knew he had other girls. But she was curious about pleasure and he gave it to her. Her parents did not force her to tie herself to this light-minded, un-reliable, delicious boy. They disliked his family—Franck-line's father knew something against Maarten's father that he would never articulate—and were content to bury the association. But the kindness and gentleness that had always been in her mother cooled and evaporated, and Franckline became like a guest politely tolerated in her own home. Her mother went through the dutiful mo-tions of serving food to Franckline's plate, of reminding her to say her evening prayers. But her soft, murmuring patter dried up near Franckline. Her every gesture ex-pressed shame that her daughter could not control her body, could not stay pious and clean. And Franckline's shame at her mother's shame spread deep into her bones, settled there like an ache. Perhaps that was when the baby inside started to die. Started its long process of dying that would be completed only outside the womb. Her mother's quiet disapproval and withdrawal was a death in itself, and Franckline's despair at it was transmitted, she is sure of it, to the child. She transgressed twice, first by making the child, then by giving it her despair, the despair that made it unable to live.

And she has been punished. Punished with a womb scraped of all the necessary ingredients for health and flowering. Yet she hopes.

(But Bernard says to her: *This is nonsense, what you tell yourself, Franckline. You can't kill a child with thoughts, with sadness. And there is no punishment: a bicornate uterus, Franckline, a simple medical fact; you were born that way.*

She knows all that, of course. Who knows better than she, with her training, her knowledge of anatomy? Yet over and over she needs him to say it to her.)

"And how are we doing here!" calls out a young, plump, fair-skinned nurse as she enters room 7. Lore looks up, relieved. The moment Franckline walked out, the room went still, like a ship when the wind shifts and dies. It felt so strange; and then Lore had gazed around at the couch against the big window and the computer monitor and the little cabinets with who knows what hidden behind them—linens, bandages, stuff to be smeared and sprayed—and down at the monstrous bed, with its white sheets and cranks and levers and her own hurt, breathing form. It was completely silent. It had made her sink and plunge for a moment, she who was never afraid of being alone. She had always known how to be alone. Yet for a moment (Franckline had left, so quickly, to go to the restroom) the edifice had shaken; she had wobbled. For several minutes she listened to her rapidly beating heart, taking long, slow breaths. But her heart would not give up its panic; it rattled on, afraid. Here is someone new, however. Perhaps she will be someone to hold onto.

"I'm all right," she says hopefully. The nurse, turning away, plucks Lore's chart from the door.

"Laura, Laura," she says. "Thirty-one, primigravida, forty weeks and two days pregnant, uh-huh, five feet nine inches, weight 179. Blood pressure, yup. Okay, Dr. Merchant checked you at 9:03 AM, fifty percent effaced, three centimeters dilated."

"It's Lore," says Lore.

"Okay," says the nurse. She gives Lore a quizzical look. "Where is your monitor?"

"I wear it once an hour. Dr. Elspeth-Chang said it was okay. I want to be able to walk around."

The nurse frowns. "We can't keep track of the baby if you don't wear it all the time."

Lore tenses at the phrase. These hospital people think *keeping track* is everything, the whole thing. "The doctor is fine with it. The other nurses have been fine with it. I understand the risks." She'd like to inform the nurse that there are risks associated with using the monitor, too—Betsy had had plenty to say about that—but this isn't the time or place for a lecture, and the nurse is clearly not going to be swayed. She still hasn't gotten close enough for Lore to read her ID tag.

The nurse scans Lore's chart again, lingering over something that must be Franckline's notation about the monitor, glances at the clock. She flips through the rest of the chart, removes Lore's birth plan, looks at the first sentence or two, then puts it back. She gazes around the room as if in search of something she can improve.

"Let me spruce up that pillow for you," she says, and although it creates an uncomfortable pressure, Lore bends forward to let the nurse—Carol: the ID tag has finally appeared in her sight line—remove the pillow and replace it. Carol presses a button and the head of the bed reclines a couple of inches.

"Could you leave the bed alone?" Lore says sharply. "I liked it the way it was." In fact she's not sure she cares either way, but what gives this woman the right to come in and change things around, get snarky about the monitor, insist her pillow needs to be plumped?

"Of course, of course," says Carol, smiling. She returns the backrest to its position.

A memory, obvious in its connection, prods at Lore. She and Asa had been in the apartment on the Upper West Side for a couple of months. They'd decorated indifferently, neither of them much interested in furniture, or things matching, so long as there was a nice bed and a few comfortable places in the living room to sit. There was a battered couch Lore had bought from her old roommates and an Ikea bookcase she and Asa had put together. Julia had a key to the place; it was Lore herself who had the idea and got it made. The apartment was closer to Julia's latest waitressing job than Julia's own; why not give her a place to grab a snack and put up her feet between shifts?

At first Asa said no. "Look, Julia and I have a complicated history. This should be our space, yours and mine." But Lore—prompted by what? A desire to please Julia and show that she trusted her? Trusted Asa?—insisted. She felt it would be mean not to offer; perhaps Julia was even expecting her to do so and would be hurt and annoyed if she didn't. All right, Asa finally agreed; let's hope she doesn't abuse it. He said Julia didn't always have *boundaries*. He didn't want to come in at night and find her hanging out.

Julia didn't abuse her right. As planned, she came only after shifts to rest up; otherwise she rang the bell and waited to be let in. But one afternoon Lore returned after school to find Julia reading a paperback and the couch in a completely different place than it had been that morning. There was a brightly colored cloth over the coffee table, with irregular splatters of reddish-brown on it. Lore couldn't tell for sure whether the splatters were old wine stains or part of the design. That was so Julia. The table where Asa and Lore ate meals was at a right angle to the kitchen pass-through rather than flush against it, and Julia had taken the chair in the bedroom where Lore threw her dirty clothes and set it up near the walled-up fireplace. Lore began to laugh in discomfort.

Julia hid her face to her eyes with the book, making a theatrically anxious expression, and asked, "Do you like it?"

Lore suppressed a tickle of irritation. The room looked, in fact, wonderful. She even liked the splattered cloth. "I do. It looks much better than before."

"You're not angry?"

"No, but you're bold, girl, you're very bold." She laughed again and knocked Julia's book from her hand so that it tumbled to the floor. Julia, who hated for her books to get roughed up, reached for it, but Lore pushed her back and straddled her, giving her phony punches while Julia put up her hands, giggling. "I wanted to give you guys a present," Julia pleaded. "It's your anniversary."

"What anniversary?" Lore climbed off, out of breath. She went to get a glass of water.

"You've been together eight and a half months."

"That's an anniversary?"

"Why not? Do you think Asa will be aggravated?"

"Asa's never aggravated by what you do."

"That's definitely not true."

"I'll tell him I like it," Lore said. The new position of the couch made the room seem more spacious. And that spaciousness made it suddenly apparent to her that the walls of the room were very bare.

"We have to put some stuff up," she said, pointing. "Here and here and here."

"No kidding. I've been so good not to say anything about it. My friend Cliff's work would look great here. He's going to be a big deal one day, I'm really convinced, but right now he's selling his paintings for almost nothing."

"Great, we'll look at them."

"I want you to have a beautiful space."

"Thank you," Lore said.

"No, I really mean it. It's important that this place look beautiful for the two of you."

Asa was in fact taken aback by Julia's redecorating. Julia and Lore had agreed in advance that he should find Lore alone when he came home, and that she should pass off the new room as her own work. But Asa didn't buy it.

"Julia did this."

"I did it, Asa. I thought it would look better this way."

"No, this is totally Julia. This thingy on the coffee table—that's Julia."

"Okay, I asked for her advice. She brought the fabric, the rest I figured out myself."

"Give me a break. This was her idea, whether you helped her or not, and I don't like it. This is our place. It shouldn't look like her. Do you get it?"

Lore, not a crier, felt something quiver inside. The idea of going back to the old room—how had she not noticed how bland, how ugly, it was?—dejected her intolerably.

"I don't see anything wrong with making things a little nicer. I don't have an eye for this stuff, and she does."

"Lore." He took her in her arms. "We can make the room nicer. We *will* make the room nicer. But Julia . . .

she needs everything to have something to do with her. So fine. But not our place, Lore. Okay?"

He tried to warn her, Lore thinks now. She'll give him that much. Or maybe he was trying to warn himself. She squirms against the backrest Carol has readjusted, trying to get comfortable again. She and Asa spent that evening pushing the couch back into position, folding up the wine-stained fabric, returning the chair to the bedroom. "At least let's put something on the walls," Lore said, and Asa answered, "Of course." That weekend they picked out some pieces at an outdoor crafts fair, and Asa didn't even bargain over the prices. But Lore never liked them as much as she was sure she would have liked the paintings by Julia's friend.

Nurse Carol putters around, watering the hibiscus on the windowsill, checking bathroom supplies. "I'm surprised they gave you a room," she says cheerfully. "You don't seem to have much going on."

Lore shrugs. She's not going to defend her right to the room.

"Well, it's slow this morning, I guess they don't mind, but if it gets busy they'll move you back to triage. Maybe that will motivate you, huh?"

"Yeah," says Lore dryly. "That will motivate me."

Silence.

"You're not much of a talker," says Carol. "I guess you can tell I'm a talker. I'm going to draw you out. Just watch."

*You've got to be kidding me*, Lore thinks. She turns her head away.

"So it's your first baby?" Carol asks as she wipes down the sink with a paper towel.

"No."

Lore looks up to see Carol squinting skeptically.

"It's my first birth, but not my first baby."

"Oh, but . . ."

"I had my first pregnancy when I was raped. I had to abort it."

"Oh," says Carol, "oh." She flushes and abruptly seats herself in the chair below the television bolted into the wall. She points herself in Lore's direction, as if to announce that she is here, she is a ready receptacle, if Lore wants to unburden herself of any details.

Now why did I say that? Lore asks herself. That was vile, she thinks.

"It's all right," she tells the nurse. "It was a long time ago."

Good God, why had she said that? But the plump little woman's friendliness had been so false, so deaf; she'd wanted to say something to puncture it. Well, *that* had certainly done it. Where is Franckline, Lore wonders? Why did I say such a thing?

It was Julia who had been raped. It happened in the lobby of the Upper West Side building where Julia and her father lived. The man had cornered her in the entryway as she fished for her key. Asa blamed himself—he would never (he told Lore) be able to feel that it was not his fault. He and his older brother and their parents lived in a different building half a block away; the Foxes and the Lisks were old friends, in and out of each other's apartments all the time. Julia and Asa had walked around the city for hours that night as they often did. They were high school seniors; it was past eleven. Generally Asa walked Julia to her door, as Morningside Heights was still a dicey neighborhood at the time. But that evening Asa was angry at Julia over her friendship with another boy in their class. "It was stupid," he told Lore. "It was nothing. But at the time I was feeling like Julia shouldn't ever pay attention to anyone but me." As they'd walked about, Julia had listened sympathetically but refused to agree to put an end to the friendship. They got to Asa's door and, miffed, he said goodnight and went inside. The way Asa remembered it, Julia hesitated, as if she wanted to ask him to continue on with her. Then she left. Julia said she didn't remember the hesitation, or even the conversation, and commented that there were other nights she'd gone home by herself, it wasn't completely unusual. But then the blows to her head made her recollections of the evening fuzzy.

Her mother by then was living in Oakland. She didn't come to see Julia after the rape. Julia told Lore this a few weeks after they met and fell into a friendship that was as swift and buoyant as a love affair. "She didn't come back to be with me or see how I was. It was my father who took care of me."

And Lore had been shocked then about Julia's mother, for she had a crush on this woman she had never met, this creator of enormous, disorienting canvases that you could see if you went to certain museums in Baltimore or Austin or Cincinnati. From far away they looked like quilts, but quilts with eerily realistic images—were there photographs pinned to the cotton batting? Closer in, you saw it was all paint. Paint had created the traditional triangles and floral patterns, as well as the grainy, spontaneous-seeming "photos" of contemporary black life and black struggle: police stopping young men in cars and confronting them on the porches of their homes, young women beaten by their boyfriends, but also family dinners and college graduations and people of all ages working at various jobs. Julia showed Lore the paintings in a large book, where the text said something or other about the artist challenging viewers' assumptions about both black folk culture and the hegemonic Western tradition of realism. Lore looked slowly through the pages. One included an enlargement of a "photo" of a woman at a console of knobs and outlets, leaning in to make an adjustment. She was seen mostly from the back, and she and the console filled nearly the whole frame. Where was she? She could equally likely have been juggling an old-fashioned telephone switchboard or managing a launch at NASA. There were no particular clues in her navy skirt suit, her neatly pulled-back hair, or her discreet pearl earrings. Lore liked that the woman was placeless and without category, and purposely avoided the text accompanying the reproduction, afraid it might explain something. The woman might be highly educated, a gender and race pioneer, or very ordinary, struggling through an everyday job. Either way, though, she was in control of something, a massive set of variables that she had mastered.

Those days looking at Dora Lisk's pictures! It was all part of the first flush of Lore's great romance—the romance of being chosen by Julia and Asa, whose friends were artists and entrepreneurs and do-gooders, people who went to galleries and political rallies and read magazines on politics and culture. Who knew people whose names appeared in the *Atlantic* and the *New York Times*—or the children of those people, at least. Lore had imagined New York City would be like this, and was surprised at how easily and quickly, after those first lonely weeks, it fulfilled her fantasy. Julia and Asa had taken her up and made her feel that she was no longer a small-town girl, a kid with a grade-C education who'd spent half of her teens and twenties at a sickbed. That she could be anyone now, could re-invent herself—although it turned out that the most exotic thing to be among these new friends was, pre-cisely, herself. They were earnest and kindly and did not mind explaining when Lore asked—there was no point in faking it—who Jacques Lacan or Rem Kool-haas was. They asked her many questions about where she'd come from and what she'd done before moving to New York, and she answered patiently, but soon she was allowed to slip blissfully into their lives and con-cerns and forget about what once had been her own.

That Julia's mother had left the family and moved all the way across the country Lore could almost un-derstand: artists were cruel, artists were selfish, oth-erwise they could not do their work. (What notions Lore had then! Or perhaps she had in fact understood something.) But Julia's mother had not come when her daughter was raped. Lore could not see Dora Lisk's work in the same way after that: the precise brush-work, the young men in cars, the family dinners.

"She said she couldn't leave the baby," Julia told Lore. Her mother had had two children with another artist after moving west, and the little one, three months old, had lung problems. Lore tried to decide whether Julia wanted her to say that this was a convincing reason or an unconvincing one. She knew that Julia's mother had rarely been in contact with her even before the rape. Julia had to this day met her half brothers only once. "One day she just gave me up and never really thought about me again," Julia said. "How does that happen?" And she touched her cheek with the tops of her fingers, a gesture she had that Lore interpreted as her way of checking her own reality, making sure that she was still there, that she was in fact the one speaking. Julia's beautiful light-brown skin, and her hair that was also a light brown from her father but coarse and kinked like her mother's. Checking to prove that the two of them had blended to make something of her, that she was not oil and water, or some other combination of elements that could not cohere.

And when the pregnancy results came back, Julia said, there was the shame associated with it being your father who brought you to the clinic, your father who had to come up close to all those bloody intimate women's concerns, who had to pick up the prescription for pain meds and watch you shuffle out of the recovery room with a big pad between your legs, and bring you your bag of clothes to change back into.

(But Lore wanted never to feel sympathy for Julia again. "There's someone I need you to meet," Julia had said, the very first day they knew each other. "My friend Asa.")

"Should I put on the TV?" asks Carol cautiously.

"No," says Lore. Her hands contract with agitation. She pushes herself off the bed and walks to the window. A mistake, she realizes—she will not be able to get back on the bed without asking Carol for help, without having to be grasped and touched by her. The sun is high in the sky but hidden now behind thick banks of gray; the lights on in the buildings opposite glow as murkily as if it were evening. An ambulance whines nearby, and she realizes it's not the first one she's heard since arriving. It pulls up and a stretcher is brought out of the back. Set back from the street as she is, she cannot make out all the details, but the figure on the stretcher appears to be a skinny, pale, long-haired man, young, younger than she. A few people stand still on the street to watch, but most go on their way.

Carol comes up beside her, too close, and waits quietly, as if hoping to be of service. Miserably, Lore watches a few flecks of snow scatter down from the sky. More will come soon, she thinks, covering the streets and making things look pretty for a while. When I leave here, she reassures herself, I will be holding my baby in my arms.

The door opens, and Franckline reenters room 7, saying her thanks to Carol. (*Of course!* the other nurse replies; *Laura is doing great, terrific patient, just shout if you need me again!*) She comes to stand by Lore. "They said snow by two," she comments. "Here it is."

Lore does not reply. *She left me*, she thinks.

"Any contractions?" Franckline asks.

Lore grunts in the negative.

"So you were waiting for me," Franckline says, smiling.

And perhaps something in Lore was in fact waiting, because as Franckline helps her back onto the bed, she feels a new cramp, moving toward her quickly, quite quickly; she will need to find her breath ahead of it. "Hands and knees . . ." she entreats Franckline, and Franckline gently guides her into position. The pain begins in her mid-back and pushes down and outward, murmuring, "Make way, make way," to her pelvis and her ribs, which fret and cry, "Impossible! Impossible!" and the muscles in her lower back contract like a fist that says, "Not today!" The contraction reaches a peak, but instead of receding persists there before mounting

61

further, pressing her harder. For a long moment Lore forgets to breathe and casts around mentally, panicked—How does one breathe? Where does breath come from? Oh, help me!—until her lungs gasp of their own accord, a quick, inefficient gasp that Lore grabs by the tail and expands, and then there is time for another breath, a long one now, and a long, deep moan. But the moan this time is not simply a moan of will and pain but a call into the emptiness: *Is anyone there?* There is a blackness spreading into her vision and she feels herself spinning in an unlit sky. *Empty, empty,* her moan cries. The moan goes on, spiraling deeper into space, and at the end of it Lore falls directly into sleep, with no sense of a transition, into a dream of gray waters, of swimming with weary arms and trying to spy the shore. When she wakes a moment later—for her wrists hurt so—she is startled by the light and color. She had been swimming somewhere—for so very long!—in which light and color did not exist. She shifts her weight carefully onto her heels and rubs each circle of bone. Her hands tremble. Quite reasonably the room reassembles itself: bed, bedsheets, television, couch, sink, computer. Solid things, a solid floor under her.

"You did that beautifully," comments Franckline, who is at the couch now, removing its cushions and stacking them at the foot of the bed. "Try leaning over these next time. They'll take the weight off your wrists."

She buckles on the fetal monitor—it's past time, she says—and offers Lore a cup of ice chips. Lore fishes out the slivers to suck on, touches her forehead with her cold, wet fingers. The universe cannot be good. A good universe could not include the forcing of her child half inch by half inch down the birth canal, its soft head squeezed misshapen by the hugging walls; could not include her own grotesque and agonized prying-open. These last months Lore has often woken in the morning aware of some fearsome fact she cannot quite place. She has groped uneasily until finally, with a stab of fear, she remembers again: The baby will have to come out. It will have to come out *that* way. She has showered and put out the things for her breakfast—toast, jam, one scrambled egg—in an attempt to blur with the ordinary facts of the day the distinct, inconceivable truth.

Sucking now, numbing her mouth, she draws a drop from an ice shard, holds it like a cold jewel, then swallows. Suck, hold, swallow. Time slows to this rhythm, the pull of her tongue, the slow warming of the drop. Nothing can happen while she sucks and holds, holds and swallows. How clever of her—to slow time, to make it wait. She pokes at another chip and pops it into her mouth. Her limbs are already forgetting the pain. But Franckline says, arranging the cushions, "The baby is determined now." Franckline seizes time by the scruff, shakes it out of its stupor, sets it going again. She seats herself on the bed. "It wants out." The clock on the wall has moved forward only a minute, to Lore's alarm and outrage. *The baby froze her face coming out.*

What was that? Who said that? Lore smells leaves burning in old metal trash cans, sees opaque skies heavy and wet around a brick school building. Tricia. She has not thought of it in years. It was when she and Tricia were in fifth grade. Tricia was telling about her big sister. Her sister's mouth and eye were pulled down forever on the right side, because the sister's baby had crushed some nerves coming out. That was how Tricia explained it. That side of the mouth and the eye would never move with the other side again. Lore saw the sister once when she dropped in for a visit, and the face was worse than she had imagined: it looked as if the still side had been smashed in a door. But Tricia said her sister said it was all worth it to have gotten Ryan, who was now three years old and knew his whole alphabet. Tricia made up a game and insisted that Lore play it: What was a baby worth more than? Was it worth more than your leg? Your eyesight? All the money you could ever get?

"It wants out," says Franckline again. But why must you repeat yourself! cries Lore silently. It, he, she—who are you, tiny destroyer, tiny suffering thing? When the sonographer asked her at twenty weeks did she want to know the sex, she said no. Let the child retain its mystery, she thought, let it be free for a while longer from life rushing in, however well-meaning, with its dreams and plans: a bow in the hair, ballet lessons, a red fire truck. She, he, it. A student she had three years ago, a second grader whose parents were Senegalese, was called Soleil. A dreamy boy who could not distinguish between his "th"s and his "d"s and who drew wonderful pictures of million-windowed buildings poking high into the sky, stick figures in every window: waving, laughing, boxing, dozing. It seemed a beautiful name for a child, boy or girl: the sun that rises to give warmth and light, a ball of burning fire.

When he learned of the baby, Asa left his messages. Lore got rid of the answering machine, deleted his e-mails without reading them. Helen Fox, Asa's mother, whom she'd always liked—formidable Helen, with her white hair and her work editing thick books on sociology and anthropology, who'd once put her veined hand on top of Lore's and said that Lore made Asa happy—Helen sent checks to her at P.S. 30, with notes in her tiny handwriting pleading with Lore to phone her, to be in touch, to say that she was all right. The checks tempted Lore, but they also humiliated her, and she threw them away. She'd wanted to reply, but what could she possibly say? That Helen had been her other mother, the one who survived? The one who taught her things about history and dance, and whom she'd liked to imagine making a grandmother? She had pictured that preoccupied, severe face broken up in fond smiles. Lore was the one who would cause that to happen.

If Asa wants to speak to me, Lore thought, he will find my address and come in person, he will take the dreaded 7 train that Manhattanites hate to take, and he will wait for me. Eventually he appeared. It was late September; he sat on the steps of the three-story building where she now lived. When he stood up he was somehow less imposing than he had been six months before. She would have said he'd lost weight except that in fact he looked bloated. She'd always liked Asa's size, the bulk of him, liked being with a man bigger than herself—taller and broader and even denser, it seemed. His largeness and solidity pinned her more securely to reality, made her feel more *there*. But now he looked hollowed out.

The evening was mild and windy; they watched a man parked near her entrance get into his car and drive away. Asa spoke carefully, evenly—he was greatly agitated. He said that she might not believe him but he'd come around to being happy about the pregnancy; he'd always wanted them to have children. She had been very wrong to keep the news from him. Naturally he would be financially responsible. More important, he would be a father to whatever degree Lore would allow. He would be part of the baby's life. He would ask nothing and give anything—except that he would not give up Julia. He kept his eyes on Lore's belly. Lore, frightened, felt him in fact capable of loving this child he had not chosen. What a temptation, to feel Asa's love, just a little, through that.

"It's not your child, Asa."

"Yes, it is. It's as much mine as yours."

"I'm saying it's *not yours*. When you were in San Francisco, I went out one night. I met a guy."

"Come on, Lore. Where did you meet this guy? What was his name?"

"I don't need to tell you."

"You're making this up. You met a guy? You, what, went back to his place? I don't believe you."

"Think what you want."

They sat in silence.

"There are tests that would tell," said Asa.

"So get tested," said Lore. He would never follow through, she was convinced of it. He was here to prove he was not altogether bad, that he could still do a right thing, and maybe he could. But he would bring the scent and touch and vibration of Julia with him, and this Lore could not bear. Julia's hair on his collar, the smell of her grassy perfumes, her laugh.

Asa was weaker than he realized. If she gave him this out, he would never seek to know for sure.

"Where is the pain mostly?" asks Franckline. "In the front or the back?"

Lore startles. The pain? Ah. "The back. All in my back."

"I can massage there for you. Along the spine, especially, and right above the sacrum. You can direct me."

"I think we should call Dr. Elspeth-Chang again."

"Soon. Let's see how quickly the next one comes."

Lore puts down the cup of ice. Her mouth aches with cold. She watches the clock. Six minutes since the last contraction. Seven. *She needs me more*, Asa said to her, the night that he told her about himself and Julia. He sobbed, saying that he couldn't deceive Lore any longer, it was too wrong, Lore was the best thing that had ever happened to him, but things with Julia went way back, he didn't claim it was healthy or right, just that it was. They were like siblings, like twins, but even more than that. They understood each other, they saw the world through the same eyes. It was as if someone had married them, long, long ago, before they could even know what that meant. He didn't know what to do! He loved Lore! But Julia!

Lore cut him off. How long had he been sleeping with her?

Nearly three years.

Asa said: "We all love each other. I know we can work it out."

"No," said Lore. "We don't all love each other. *Work it out?*" She now saw why he had confessed—not so he could make a choice, but to get her permission not to. He wanted things to go on just as they had, but with Lore knowing and agreeing to it. He wanted Lore's reliability and sanity, the ease of their life together. And he wanted her so that Julia would not leave him again for the fourth or seventh time. Oh, Asa and Julia did go far back. Asa had kissed her behind the piano in kindergarten. They had slept in each other's rooms when they were in grade school. He had dropped her half a block from her apartment one night. *She needs me more.* Julia had bought Lore as a pimp might, made a gift of her to Asa, to them both. How stimulating it must have been, Lore thought, the three of them strolling along Columbus Avenue or sunning at Jones Beach or driving up to Bear Mountain for a hike, how Lore's love for them must have acted like a revivifying draft for their old, tangled romance. How deliciously illicit it must have made their need. And how stupid and arrogant Lore had been, to believe that she could take her pleasure of both of them, yet Asa could remain completely her own. The bliss, for so long, of that self-deception. Julia and Lore spooning atop a pile of coats at a party, dozing, while Asa talked on in the living room. Or Asa would say something that annoyed Julia, and Julia, slender Julia, would tackle him; he'd fake a fall, Lore would pile on. They'd roll and punch at each other like preschoolers, laughing, grabbing hair, baring teeth. Asa's hand on Julia's belly, Julia's fingers grazing his mouth: were these knowing promises of what would be redeemed on another day?

Imagine having spoken of any of this to Diana or Marjorie. Lore would have seen, behind their careful words, how appalled they were: could she really have been so clueless? But it had been exquisite: the touch of her lover, the touch of her friend. Before this her heart and her hands had been devoted to the body of a sick and dying woman, with its bruises and sores and bad smells. She is proud of having cradled and eased her mother until the end. But it had left her so very hungry.

She had colluded, in short, and all Asa was asking was that she continue to collude with eyes open. It struck her that Julia might have urged Asa to make his confession. Perhaps she had been growing bored of their stealth affair and was looking for a new drama. "Do this for me, for us," she might have said, daring him.

And why not? Wouldn't it be natural, this next step? But Lore recoiled. Not, she realized, because of any great moral objection. She could envision the new arrangement perfectly well. But she was too proud. She was, quite obviously, the variable in the equation. One day Julia would tire again and move to eject her; her X would be replaced by someone else's Y or Z. Asa would protest, perhaps, but then he would agree. Oh, he would agree. But even imagining this injury was not the worst. The worst was to acknowledge how greedy she had been, how like Julia she actually was. One lover had not been enough for her. The only difference between her and Julia was that she wasn't clever enough to have orchestrated the setup; she'd had to be swept into it, led.

"Go to her," Lore said. She was frightfully calm, except for the urgent need to have Asa leave the apartment, vanish from her sight. She was silently nearly hysterical in her desire to push him out the door. She wished there were more locks to lock: a hundred locks to lock behind him. As soon as she was alone she fell into a deep sleep, and in the morning she went to work as usual, thinking and feeling as little as possible. On her return she set about methodically destroying every memento of their lives together: photos from parties and evenings at home, the crafts-fair art, books Asa or Julia had introduced her to, any clothing bought or worn in their presence, even refrigerator clippings and scribbles on notepads. She left behind the plates and glasses, the kitchen tools. A few of her oldest items of clothing and her toiletries were all she threw into her suitcase. She was leaving with no more than she had brought with her to the city something over four years ago. In between had been a dream so vivid and compelling it had seemed real, but it was no surprise to wake up and find that she was alone again. She knew how to live lightly—she had always lived lightly. Her mother had lived lightly. People like them never accumulated much.

Eleven minutes. The smell of rubbing alcohol, new gauze. Lore looks up. A hallucination of sorts, for nothing has been opened, nothing moved; Franckline is sitting patiently at the computer desk, filling out paperwork.

No, people like them never accumulated much, only culled a little corner of the world to call their own, then moved on when trouble pushed them aside. Greenwich Village, Lockport, Hobbes Corners—more than one house there, but in each Lore's mother bent over the lilies in the stony yard. She sat at the sewing machine, sewing Lore's skirts for school. Two females, doing what females do: getting by. Had Lore missed having a father? friends had sometimes asked. Julia had asked. Lore always said no. As a child she had not been quite sure what fathers were for. Money, one would think. But her friends with fathers at home seemed to live not very differently than she and her mother did. Possibly worse—men tended to spend on hunting and bowling outings, and drink.

When Lore's mother was dying and doped up on morphine, she spoke about being a dancer in New York City. Some sort of troupe that contained girl-friends named Celeste and Patty. Bright-red skirts and castanets. There was no way to know if this had really happened, or if it was a fantasy brought on by the drugs. Her mother spoke slurrily of picking blueberries by a country lake, of finding at a flea market an embroidered blouse threaded with ribbons. "The place was so crowded and dirty," she said. "But I found what I wanted."

How naive Lore had been, despite being the daughter of a father no one spoke of, despite the strange, incomplete conversations at her mother's deathbed; how again and again she was caught up short by the discovery that other people had stories they didn't tell, or told stories that weren't entirely true. How mostly you got odd chunks torn from the whole, impossible truly to understand in their damaged form. She glances at Franckline.

Who is she, what are her stories, what does she tell and not tell? Once upon a time, Franckline arrived here from another country: there, surely, is at least one story, a story of ambition or love or flight. Is she married? (Lore quickly scans Franckline's hand. Yes.) Does she have children? Are they sweet-tempered, mischievous, shy, gregarious? Where does she live, what objects fill her home? Has she ever been betrayed by someone?

Thirteen minutes.

The girl watches the clock, and Franckline can sense her spirits plummeting. She has lost track of the monitor, and Franckline doesn't remind her. Given the slowdown in the contractions, she wants to hear the steady thumping and be able to read the regular spikes and decelerations on the printout. In the meantime, what to do for Lore? Franckline might see if she could borrow a book from one of the nurses for her, or a magazine. But she is sure that Lore would wave them away. Perhaps if Franckline offered to read to her. A few of the patients like to be read to by friends or family members. Franckline listens in, trying to expand her notion of what her adopted language might be applied to. These are usually poems that Franckline finds obscure but pleasantly rhythmic, or Bible passages that she knows better in French but enjoys hearing transmuted into the chunky mouthfuls that make up English. Last week a woman read to her sister from a novel about Russians at a great formal dance, princesses and dukes and so on. The two of them got into a lively discussion about the attractiveness of two different types of females, the girlish and the womanly. The pregnant woman said most men preferred the girlish. Her sister said they just pretended to, but really wanted the womanly. Then the patient sighed and asked her sister to put the book away and said she just wished the goddamn baby would come.

If—when—Franckline has this baby, she will not have her sister by her side. Gizelle, the only of her siblings she nearly stayed in Ayiti for. And, had she done so, would the ice in her mother's heart have one day melted, would her aunties and cousins again have felt like the very thumbs and fingers of her hands? But she had been too young to understand about time—time seemed then so large and heavy, a boulder that would crush her. She could not stay and be ground under. She had no idea that time could ever move swiftly, as it does now, that people and their feelings might eventually change. Manman died ten years ago. Franckline had not been there, had not even known until weeks later, when Gizelle tracked her down. Gizelle will know when this child is born. There are neighbors with cell phones now; the country is not as far away as it once was.

The child might mean a return to Basin Rouge, her village, to see Gizelle and her brother and her other sisters after all these years. She and Bernard have been to Port-au-Prince twice, to visit his mother and other relatives, but Franckline refused to travel to her home village. Her sister Athalie had written: *Papa says you killed Manman. You, the oldest, abandoned us.* But perhaps if she brought her father a grandchild to hold, he might forgive her. And Bernard, with his respectful ways, and his kindnesses, would win everyone over, even the brothers-in-law. They would not be able to help being impressed by his new clothes, his education, the life he and Franckline are living in New York City, with an apartment all to themselves on a street planted with rhododendrons and azaleas. They will bring gifts: new sneakers, deflated soccer balls, talcum powder, cologne.

Sixteen minutes.

"Maybe the TV," says Lore.

"Very good." Franckline points the remote at the television. Two women and a man coalesce from a blurry panel of color. At first there's no sound. The women sit on a couch and the man—the host, apparently—is behind a desk. The women, dressed in tight sleeveless sheaths and high-heeled pumps, laugh frantically over something the man has said, throwing

themselves over their laps and then throwing themselves back, flinging their long hair behind them. The
women lean and laugh, their mouths enormous, open,
glistening things, their shoe heels pointed as skewers.

Franckline pushes at the volume button and the
conversation rises into the room.

"... *tried to make the tacos* ..."

"... *food poisoning! He said he'll never trust me again* ..."

(And then male laughter: *haw haw haw haw haw*.)

Lore is staring moodily at the screen, as if wounded
by the banter of the women and the host egging it
on. Franckline wonders if she ought to find another
channel, but they will all be the same: laughter and
loud voices, guns and car chases, at best a religious
lecture. Merchandise spinning on a platform. Perhaps
that would be all right: earrings and bracelets nestled
in gray velvet, glinting in the bright TV lights. Sometimes, in the evening, tired from work, Franckline
watches Home Shopping Network or QVC with the
sound turned low. If you know you are never going
to buy anything, it can be soothing to watch the glittering items offered one after the other. You probably enjoy them for nearly as long as the people who
buy them do. Bernard believes that the television for
anything but the news and the financial reports is a
waste of time, and occasionally Franckline has to fix

him with a look and say that perhaps he doesn't ever need waste and forgetfulness but that she, at least for tonight, does.

"... *a tattoo* where? ..."

"... *no, darling, I won't show you* ..."

(*Haw haw haw haw haw!*)

Nineteen minutes since Lore's last contraction. Franckline feels a pulsing in her groin—not quite a pain, perhaps, or, yes, a pain. Is she imagining pain into being by fearing it? At the library in Flatbush, on the computers there, she has looked at the images of bicornate uteruses, pinkly meaty, split like a wishbone. The two petal-like chambers, the gestational sac residing in one. Her baby is growing in the left chamber. The hospital doctors say there's a reasonable chance the chamber will expand enough to allow the baby to grow to term, especially since Franckline has already borne a full-term child, but they don't want to make promises. She can't help at times picturing the child running out of room, the head pushing against the uterine wall, or the cervix giving way and the unfinished life spilling out.

Snow falls outside the window, not heavy, not light, steady and wet-looking, small splatters of moisture rather than neat dry flecks. The evening she met Bernard he spoke of snow, the delicate, floating wonder of it, and the tall hills that stayed on the ground for weeks and did not disappear. They were at his mother's table. Bernard had found her on the steps of the Port-au-Prince Cathedral, where she sat, footsore and very hungry, having wandered for hours in the city. She had lasted six months at home, trying not to see her lost baby in the face of every child. She had wept so compulsively, so unendingly, that even her aunt Thérèse, her favorite, who always indulged her, slapped her and said it was time to behave herself, to stop spitting at fate. She would have another child, many more, Tante Thérèse told her, at the right time, but Franckline wondered who would take her as his woman in her disgrace. Her value had been greatly reduced. Would she be made to join with someone she hated, who disgusted her? And in any case the thought of more children did nothing to numb the ache; it was *that* child, the silent child, the one she had come to know so well over the months she had carried him—his kicks and hiccups and slumbers—that she longed for. *That* child would never be born again, not in that body, on that day. She had been meant to be ashamed of him but he had been immune to her shame, had been something great and new and clean, for all the days he had lived.

She left home one day in late spring. She had turned eighteen the week before. A woman wrapped in dirty tatters leaned against one of the cathedral arches, muttering and occasionally, sharply, calling out the word "Father!" like a curse. Franckline had spent nearly all of her money on a series of tap-taps to the city, and she had no place to stay. She had thought, foolishly, that she could sleep in a park or behind the Presidential Palace unmolested, but the eyes and gait of the men on the street made her understand that this was not so. Now, about 10:00 PM, a man approached her and said he had a room for the night, did she need one? She suspected what sort of payment this might involve but she was panicky and hungry and she was already, in the mind of those she had left behind, spoiled. Would it matter so much? But before she could rise to join the man, Bernard was there, telling the man to *Al fè rout ou*, to leave his sister alone. The man shrugged skeptically and moved away. Like a bad spirit he vanished into the dark. Bernard asked Franckline if she wanted something to eat, and bought her a large plate of goat *fritay* from a street vendor. She supposed he might be merely another, cleaner, version of the man who had offered her the room, particularly after he said she couldn't stay out like this for the night, he would take her to his mother. But she didn't think so. His eyes didn't seem to have the same narrowed appraisal in them. His gentleness did not appear to be a fraud.

He did in fact take her to his mother, not far from the center of the city. She was a tall woman with glasses and a commanding air. She served Franckline—aware that she had not bathed for two days—spiced cocoa and fresh pineapple, and Bernard talked about Miami and New York, both cities he had studied in; he planned to go into banking or finance. He described the snow in the north, where they had family, how surprisingly light it was when you scooped it into your hands. And yet it was heavy enough to make roofs tumble down. He did not talk about how, within days, it blackened and crusted on the sidewalks and turned into gray slush in the streets. Franckline discovered that only once she was in Brooklyn herself. The banks that grew up by the sides of the road frightened her; she found it sinister the way they buried lost things, items revealed only months later: a doll's arm, a stamped envelope, a child's pair of pants. When Franckline passed by those banks, all she could think of was the refuse hidden inside.

She did not believe Bernard had omitted the snow's despoilation to make a better story, to entice her. More likely he simply did not think of it. What mattered was the beauty life presented you with; ugliness was incidental, transient. The essence of snow was to be beautiful; therefore, in all of Bernard's stories about snow, it was beautiful. Bernard's mother showed Franckline where she could bathe, and put her to bed in sheets that were wonderfully stiff and clean. In the morning there was hot coffee and fresh bread and eggs. Bernard had already left for his job delivering crates of cereals and soap.

A knock on the labor room door, but the one who knocked doesn't wait, opens the door and strides in. It is a tall, broad, youngish man in a dark overcoat dusted, like his hair, with snow, snow that seems to have tumbled right out of Franckline's recollections to moisten his nose and eyebrows. He strides past Franckline toward Lore. He is carrying an enormous white stuffed panda with a store tag still dangling from one ear. He stops abruptly and turns back to Franckline.

"Judith Cooley's room?" he asks. "I thought this was Judith Cooley's room?"

On the bed Lore is holding her gown together with one hand, with the other arranging it to cover her thighs. Franckline steps between her and the man to better block her from his view.

"Check with the charge nurse," she says briskly. "Out the door and back to your right, the big desk."

*"Coming up at four: Laura Bush's top barbecue recipes!"*

"I'm her brother," says the man, not moving, as if hoping that by staying longer he can lessen his blunder. "I just drove in from Rochester."

"That's all right," says Franckline. *Go!* she thinks. "Down the hall to your right and talk to Marina."

Lore watches the panda (WELCOME BABY, its white T-shirt had read) bob out of sight and disappear; the door closes with a resounding bang. She curls onto her side, her knees drawn up, her fists tensed against her belly, the obstructing cords from the fetal monitor enraging her. She'd thought for a moment . . . there was that familiar-looking black wool coat, a familiar height and dark hair; she'd believed for a moment . . . she will not say it! But her thoughts betray her. *Asa.* Asa with his arms full of childish whimsy; Asa whom she had forbidden to see her again. The man had stood there; she had felt the shock of familiarity in her belly and her groin; her heart had moved with giddy velocity toward his figure.

She curls over the baby, protecting it from her deranged vision, apologizing: *A mistake, my little one, a momentary fit, he is not good enough for you, not good enough for us, and he is never coming anyhow, and we do not need him, we do not need him!*

And the baby moves within her, pressing, replying: *Get up, get up! For I am coming!* For the baby does not care about *him.* It has nothing to do with him, nor with her, either, not really, not now. It has only one task, to press forward. It cannot help it. It will tear her if it must. It will, if it needs to, freeze a mouth and an eye.

The pressure in her pelvis expands. And there, by the bed, before Lore has said anything, or is even aware that she has made a sound, stands Franckline. The nurse props her up and she leans over the pillows now stacked at the foot of the bed, which do just what Franckline promised. They take the weight off her dangling wrists and hands and allow her to feel almost gravityless, to concentrate on the only facts that matter: the prying-open of the exit to her womb and the heavy weight of Franckline's hands. Franckline massages her back, her strong thumbs pushing into the narrow pockets around Lore's spine and into her sacrum, the pain of this pressure breaking up the pain coming from within. Her throat loosens to let out more voice.

"... *biggest feet in the universe* ..."

"... *I can top that one* ..."

Lore's growls drown out the television voices, render the action on the screen pantomime. The figures on the couches laugh, flap, lean toward and away from each other. They perform for nobody. But when Lore is silent again, their conversation rises and swoops into the room. "*Well, I'd never let* my *husband* ..."

"Could you turn off the TV?" Lore asks. Franckline picks up the remote and gives the TV a zap. The shiny women and the smooth man vanish.

It was a full minute, Franckline tells Lore. Lore should be proud of herself. The nurse takes a chance and strokes the girl's forehead. While attending to Lore, her own pain disappeared. Perhaps she had indeed imagined it.

Lore's forehead is hot; her stomach churns threateningly. The sensation gradually passes, and her eyes flutter closed. In a couple of minutes she wakes, feeling calm. She turns her head. Franckline is sitting quietly by the bed, her hands folded. Lore fixes on the nurse's cross, a small gold piece hanging from a gold chain. She again has the impulse to ask Franckline about herself but she is tired, she thinks she won't be able to listen, and besides, stories are too hard, are almost always convoluted and do not tell the thing you really want to know. What she wants to know is what Franckline does in the moments when she despairs. Does she ever despair? Surely—that cross—she prays, and praying is something Lore does not believe in, or even know how to do.

Another contraction. Though Lore focuses as usual on her voice, on expelling sound as the pain rises, she has the sensation this time of standing slightly outside of herself, and she is aware, now, of other sounds in the room: the speeded-up heartbeat the monitor broadcasts (*lub-lub-lub-lub-lub-lub-lub*), Franckline's deep, heavy breathing as she presses hard into Lore's back. She is fascinated to hear the baby's heartbeat slow as the pain recedes. There are sounds of the wind outside, erratic rattlings of the window, and a dog's sharp bark, one-two-three-four, stopping abruptly. Footsteps in the hallway outside.

Then she is asleep again.

When she wakes she has the sense that it has been several minutes. Her body is quiet; she detects no pain moving in. But it can't be far away. When another few minutes pass and nothing happens, she tells Franckline she would like to get on her feet. Franckline helps her off the bed, holds her arm until Lore is steady. Lore walks back and forth a few paces to restore the sense of ground under her, then moves to the window. The sky is still dark and the snow doesn't look as pretty as she had hoped; rapid footfalls are already disrupting the thin layer and pushing it into the street, where cars that seem to be driving too fast return it from their tires as dirty spray. She watches as another ambulance pulls up, this one silent for some reason, but turns away before she can see what its back doors will discharge.

The pain hasn't abandoned her. It is coming toward her again, and she reaches out for Franckline.

"Show me your hand," says Franckline. It is past three. Lore lies on her side. There was a good half hour, forty minutes, of more frequent contractions, and now she is waiting again. The dark air outside washes in and mutes the bright fluorescents, creating an under-the-sea effect. A short time ago she cried out in frustration and disbelief, and Franckline said that some labors are just like this, start and stop, start and stop. "But the baby comes eventually, believe me," she said.

She rests Lore's palm in her own and tells her that the finger with the ring seems to her more swollen than before. "Your blood pressure could be up—I want to check that. We need to take this off," she pronounces firmly, touching the silver band. "Is it something special?"

"No," says Lore.

"You haven't wanted to take it off."

Franckline gazes down at her, waiting. Lore likes her silences; she can look at her then, study her long, smooth face that has a small scar below the left eye.

"We can save it," Franckline assures her. "They will cut it in just one place, and you can have it repaired later."

The ring cost Lore a good deal, nearly three hundred dollars. Of course that was much less than Asa must have spent on the one he bought her, a teardrop emerald flanked by two diamonds. She flushed it down the toilet six weeks later, the day after she sent him back to Julia. It could have been sold for good money.

"Lore. Can you feel it when I press your finger? I didn't think so."

She never figured out how Asa paid for the ring. Probably only a loan from his parents could have made the purchase possible, but at the same time she can't imagine proud Asa ever asking them. She was appalled when he first gave it to her—she was even more frugal, in some ways, than he was. He had come home with a louder than usual clatter of shoes and satchel, gripping the day's takeout coffee that he wasn't going to finish—because tossing it would be profligate. He seemed hyped up. They sat down to bowls of a lentil soup they'd made over the weekend and he nudged the ring box in her direction. She opened it and looked at him. He was silent.

"Is this an engagement ring?"

"Mmm," he said.

A proposal seemed uncharacteristically old-fashioned of him. She'd figured the inevitable decision to marry would be a joint one, something they'd come to one night after a talk about the apartment and their bills. That was their style. Lore's first thought was that the money he'd spent on the ring would have better gone toward their wedding. But when she started to say this, and to protest that he should return it for something simpler, he became agitated, and told her that if he couldn't spoil her over an engagement ring, whenever would he?

She should have been suspicious then. In fact she was suspicious. When had Lore ever needed or wanted to be spoiled? When had their lovers' vocabulary ever included the word *spoiling*? One evening a few weeks earlier, she and Asa and Julia were sitting over dinner in the apartment, and she was pricked by a wordless thought. She looked from Asa to Julia and back again. The thought escaped her, and what occurred in its place was that Asa and Julia were looking more and more alike. People had sometimes taken them for brother and sister despite the difference in their physiques—because of the olive skin, the long narrow noses, the curly hair. Their height, their long fingers and the way they had of thrusting them up in the air when excited. People guessed: Jewish? Black? Italian? But related to each other, surely. Now it seemed to Lore that even their ears had the same shape, and that they cocked their heads at the same angle and cut up their vegetables in the same slow, overly attentive way. The words coming out of their mouths, for several fugue-like minutes, had the same timbre, the same intonations. And then Lore came out of it and reached for another helping of spaghetti bolognese, and took a sip of red wine.

Lore had flushed the emerald ring away, her pride beating loudly in her ears, when she could have sold it. Then she bought herself this silver band, in an absurdly expensive boutique in Soho, to celebrate the fact that she did not need a fiancé to have a ring. The woman in the shop explained that the pattern was Native American and meant everlasting love and life. "It will bring you good luck. You see how the L shapes repeat? There's no beginning or end."

Now she would be her own fiancé; she would marry herself. She would be both father and mother to this child. It was, really, one of the most ordinary stories in the universe.

She waits with dumb patience as Franckline applies the pressure cuff and puffs it tight around her upper arm. The reading is normal, 120 over 90, but Franckline takes it twice. Then she says that the ring must still come off, she is going to call an orderly. Let her take it off then, Lore thinks. She commits an exaggerated shrug of surrender. She is tired. She is very tired. The ring, Franckline has promised, can be repaired.

"And I'll check in with Dr. Elspeth-Chang," Franckline says, to reward her.

This time Lore closes her eyes so as not to notice the absence in the room, the fact that Franckline is gone. The place behind her eyes winks with pricks of light, interior stars, and, slowly, location retreats. There is no room around her, no hospital, no busy street with cars shushing by—just the faint sound of a horn, blocks away. She is untethered, a blurry presence smudged across a dense atmosphere. How good to be this blurred thing within a muted hum. The horn sounds again. The ache in her neck dissolves; her heavy belly is a great buoyant ball. How, mostly, she had liked moving through the streets of the city, even in her fatigue, with the great belly before her. Her slow, ponderous strides, and the way knots of people sidestepped and fanned out to give her way. Some timeless instinct that people still had of respect and humility toward a woman carrying new life. Lore stopped into the small, cunning baby-clothing shops on Madison Avenue— she could afford almost nothing in them—and tears misted her eyes at the tiny organic-cotton onesies and socks. There were embossed wooden blocks and certified toxin-free bottles and swirls of board books that would expose your baby to fascinating colors and textures for twenty dollars apiece. Lore thought it all ridiculous, a way of extorting money out of people who had too much of it, but at the same time she longed for all this apparatus of purity and improvement. Less ridiculous to her was the purity of the birth itself: the dignity of labor without intrusion—without monitors,

injections, forceps, stitches. She painted in her mind
a picture of a mattress on the floor and candles on
the windowsill. Quiet music playing in a corner, and
strong hands. A baby's lone wail in the busy silence.
Then she erased that picture because who would stay
up with her, whose would be the hands? It would have
to be the hospital and its dark competencies after all.
But still she would keep her child and herself as safe
from the meddling world as she could. Offered the
AFP test and the Tay-Sachs, she refused. She would accept this child in whatever condition it arrived. Dr.
Elspeth-Chang shook her head. A single mother, Lore
might be financially ruined by caring for a child with
a serious disability. Lore replied that she knew how to
make do, had come from people who always made do.

So she ate stir-fried vegetables and brown rice, and
sitting on the toilet she clenched and unclenched
her pelvic muscles to prevent episiotomy. One of the
cunning stores on Madison carried a book called *The
Birth Plan*, which Lore bought. She read it and took
pages of notes. She had thought already about the epidural and rooming in, but it seemed there were many
other things to consider—should one allow the Vita-
min K injection? The erythromycin drops? Whenever
she thought of her Soleil emerging from the warmth
of her body into cold air and brisk professional hands

and the terror of being moved swiftly through open space, a pang seized her throat, and she shut her eyes against the pictures. In accepting the hospital she had accepted these insults to Soleil—the air, the hands, the flailing—but she would spare Soleil what pain she could. She spent long hours after school reading in *The Birth Plan* about typical hospital procedures— what was necessary and what might be less so—and she composed her instructions. It was satisfying to draft and redraft, to hone her desires. Detail did not bore her. Detail was power. Child care for Soleil would cost $1,200 a month, once she went back to work. Diapers and other supplies were budgeted for the first year at $750, formula and food at $800, clothing at almost none, since a colleague at P.S. 30 planned to deed Lore her toddler's old sleepers and unisex overalls and Ts.

She dozes. A great umbrella opens, its spines blooming outward, but one spine is broken and the black fabric flaps up and down . . . Now Franckline is speaking to her. With an effort Lore concentrates, wakes. Dr. Elspeth-Chang would like to try to finish seeing her scheduled afternoon patients. "There's not much for her to do until you're fully dilated," says Franckline. "But you're moving along. Do you want the resident to check you again?"

Lore declines drowsily. Keep that doctor's dirty fingers out of me, she thinks. She holds her hand before her eyes and looks at the flesh pinched deeply by the silver ring. I suppose I could do without one finger, she decides.

Franckline rises and, murmuring something Lore doesn't catch, ducks into the bathroom at the front of the labor room. The door shuts with a click. Gone again! cries Lore silently. But it is only the bathroom, she reminds herself, and people must close the door when using the bathroom. Still, why should all these people come and go, come and go, nurses and doctors and men with snow in their hair, but she must lie on the bed, beached and passive? She too will go, she thinks. She will get up and walk out the door. This is not a prison or a reformatory, she has the right. She pushes herself upright and does her best to arrange the awkward gown, grips her hospital slippers with firm toes. One thing she learned very young was that if you carried yourself as if you had business, as if your presence somewhere was legitimate, people didn't notice if you were in the wrong place or doing the wrong thing. At Our Lady of Sorrows she wore socks that were too short, or in non-approved colors, and if she pretended to herself that she was dressed according to code, none of the nuns seemed able to see. So now she walks the hallway without her nurse. She takes the opposite direction this time, and feels an outsize excitement at the thought of learning what might lie beyond the maternity ward in this direction, not Pulmonary but something else, some other troubled part of the body, and rooms filled with people suffering in an entirely different way. Old and young, poor and rich, sick and sicker. Young and rich did not keep you from being cut down, not always. Her mother (not rich, but not old either) had died at forty-five. She lay in the hospital bed in the house in Hobbes Corners, her mouth drawn into an oblong, and an odor to her breath that Lore would know forever after as the odor Death sent when it knew it had won its fight to take you.

At the funeral, which Lore had arranged—small: her mother's family, awkward and treating Lore like a stranger; a smattering of work colleagues and neighbors—and paid for with money left for this purpose, she looked down at her mother's face, relaxed of some of its characteristic lines, and thought that here lay the only person who would ever truly understand her, the only person she would ever care to be close to.

"We're the same like that," Julia told her, the day they'd met. "Both of our mothers are dead." Julia told lies that had a certain poetic truth to them, and that she believed were true when she said them. Another time she claimed that as a child she'd gone blind for three months from hysteria, not wanting to see her parents fighting. (Asa, when asked, smiled and disputed the tale.) Julia and Lore were in the cafeteria at MoMA. It was a Friday evening in February, and Lore had been in New York City for six weeks. She was twenty-six years old and her mother had died in a final relapse in late November. It had been difficult to jump into her job midyear, to pick up the caseload that Mrs. Butler, injured in a car accident, had left behind. P.S. 30 was overheated, and by day's end Lore was desperate to walk in the open air, even though the weather was bitter. She bypassed her subway stop and kept moving uptown, until she could feel her face stinging and her right hand—she had lost one of her gloves that morning—become numb. She stopped at a street vendor and paid four dollars for new gloves. Cutting west in the Fifties, she saw a line snaking out of the Museum of Modern Art and, when she asked what people were waiting to see, was told that it was a free-admission Friday. She got in line, joining the other shivering, jiggling bodies, grateful to have a reason not to go back yet to her apartment in the West 100s (also overheated, and shared with two impossibly messy recent college graduates, one of whom had two cats). The line moved slowly, and by the time she had gained entry to the museum she felt hungry. A look at the prices in the crowded cafeteria convinced her to stick to a cup of coffee. She asked a young woman with long, tightly curled hair if the empty chair next to her was taken. Julia shook her head and gestured that Lore should sit down. Her eyes, which blinked rapidly, were green. She was like a sea creature, sylph-like, somehow rippling and glittering. She was reading an expensive fashion magazine, which she put companionably aside.

"A speech teacher," Julia breathed, upon asking what Lore did for a living, as if it were the most fabulous occupation she had ever heard of. "You help people, all day long."

"Well," said Lore, shy at the attention this elegant girl was paying to her. She allowed that she probably did help people—children, anyway. She felt good about her work. Julia said that she herself was useless, a painter, which was about the most selfish thing that anyone could be. She dabbed up the last crumbs of her croissant with her finger.

"Do you like it? What do you like about it?" she asked, and Lore, who hadn't been asked this question since coming to the city (and had rarely been asked it before), found herself speaking about the pleasure of taking a child step by step through the necessary adjustments, the small changes of jaw and teeth and breath, that enabled them to be heard by the world. For every child you had to find the key; the exercises or instructions that helped one did not help another. You had to be intimate with them—to peer inside their mouths, place a finger on their gums. You had to touch their tender throats, test the vibrations at the backs of their necks. These were children who garbled their desires and their protests, and the grown-ups in their world did not listen to them as they should, because you do not listen well to someone who cannot be plain.

"Do you love them?" Julia asked, and this was something people never asked at all. Often they told her she *must* love children, to work with them so closely. Lore paused. She said she wasn't sure. She *liked* them. She thought she'd loved a few of them, over time. She said that people who went on about how adorable children were never spent all day with them. Children were in fact ferocious little animals, sharp and canny and hurt and eager to inflict hurt themselves, who were trying to get what they needed in life. And she helped them to articulate those needs. That was why she did it. That, and because she seemed to have a knack for it.

Julia said: "I wish I could like children. But they scare me. They always seem to want something, and I don't know what it is."

It was like that, from the beginning: the way they spoke. Lore had never known anyone who behaved the way Julia did, who went directly to the important thing, and enabled you to talk about it too. So that you never wanted to go back to the ordinary type of conversation, which was all mask, all a way of never figuring out what really wanted to be said.

Lore listens for pain, feels nothing. She can sense, beyond the pale-yellow walls of the corridor, the deepening of late afternoon into dusk. She follows behind an older man in a neat polo shirt and trim slacks, tensing as they pass the desk at the end of Maternity, but the nurse there doesn't look up fully, just buzzes both her and the man through. A sign tells her she's in Radiology, and she stops to take in a large framed picture. A shoreline somewhere or other, gray-yellow rocks, pink-blue water. There are little flecks meant to be people at leisure: walking along the sand, wading into the surf. One of the flecks (she moves closer) is a mother bending down to hand a fleck child an ice cream cone. Lore's mother had a picture much like it, though smaller, which she hung just inside the front door in each of their Hobbes Corners homes. She said if she had all the money in the world she would buy a beach house and lie in the sun all day. (Yet she never learned how to swim, never once went with Lore to the ocean.) *Sentimental*, Julia would have said of that picture—and of this one, too. Julia had strong opinions about certain kinds of paintings and movies and rooms. She despised easy beauty. Beauty, she said, should always have something ugly and off-kilter in it, something true. The paling sun in the picture is more than halfway down the sky; it is that moment in a long, hot day where the light cools and the sweat on one's neck and shoulders dries, and one is sated and sleepy from the sun sunk deep into one's bones. Lore leans in to see the name on the plate by the picture: Thomas Eddington, 1993.

After the cafeteria, Lore got to see the kind of art Julia liked. Not oceans and ice cream cones. Fifth floor, Austrian Expressionism: pictures by George Grosz and Otto Dix and Egon Schiele. A riot of thick paint, weird illumination, clashing colors. Egon Schiele looked out at Lore with the deep-bored, jutting-browed, demonic eyes of his self-portrait; there was something sinister in the tuft of hair just visible at his armpit. He clutched his skull; his white fingernails accused her. Julia was very still as she stood in front of each picture. Lore looked at Julia's lovely face, her sloe eyes, next to the rabid reds and greens and purples of the canvases, and was visited with the knowledge that this was what Julia looked like inside, smeared and inflamed. She understood. She took Julia's hand, squeezed it. Julia squeezed back. I have a friend, Lore thought.

"Ahoy!" calls some wag, a white-haired orderly trying to catch her attention; his stretcher needs to come through. Lore steps to the side to let pass a figure so covered up with sheets and scrub cap and tubing that Lore can't tell whether it is a man or a woman. A woman, she decides. She drops her head in unconscious respect. One long-fingered hand, all knuckles and joints, rests atop the sheet; the rest of the form, glimpsed underneath, is tiny and emaciated. Is the woman alive or dead? Alert or sedated? As a child, Lore was fascinated by the story in a book of Greek myths about a young man who appealed to Hera for eternal life. Hera, malicious, granted his wish literally. He had asked for eternal life, but he had neglected to ask never to grow old. And so the years went by and the man aged; his back became bent, his skin discolored and sagged, his limbs shriveled and eventually gave way. Centuries passed and he became smaller and drier and more withered until finally he was no larger or sturdier than a grasshopper, and Hera brought him to Olympus and put him in a little cage, where he was forced to emit his dry rasps for her entertainment for eternity.

Perhaps the woman under the sheets was once very young and beautiful (at least, she would have been young) and had wished for what the young man had wished for, and now here was her recompense. A quiet muttering rises from beneath the sheet and Lore imagines that the old woman is dreaming of herself with beautiful, lavender-tipped iridescent wings; she is singing all day long for a goddess. It might be lovely if we could have immortality even via hallucination, even the hallucinated immortality of a hallucinated insect.

*Sentimental,* Julia repeats, of Thomas Eddington's painting. *Okay, okay,* Lore replies, rattled, and turns away. Who is she to argue? She is not a maker of things; she does not have that talent. She cannot draw or paint; she plays no instrument; her writing is blunt and practical. Her creative gift, if she has one, is to help children learn how to speak. Into that she pours her patience, her instinct, her ingenuity. *That's all right with you, isn't it, little one?* she asks, touching her belly. *Anyway, it's what you got.*

She moves on. There are open rooms with big machines; one is being wiped down by a young man with a face mask hanging loose under his chin. He smiles at her, as if they know each other, and, caught off guard, Lore smiles back. *Suppose,* she thinks. *Suppose it was him I'd sat down next to at the museum . . .* But she is carrying the great weight of a different path and of someone else's child, and she walks on, her skin warm, her fingers tingling a little.

When Lore and Julia stopped back at the cafeteria for more coffee, putting off parting, Julia told Lore that there was someone she wanted her to meet. "My friend Asa. He needs a girlfriend."

"And I just happened to show up?"

"No! You would be so right for him. I have the funniest feeling."

Asa, Julia explained, was her oldest friend. He was handsome and funny and smart and unaccountably unattached. They'd known each other since they were born, their parents had been close at the university. Asa's and Julia's fathers were professors of history there; Asa's mother worked at the university press. Julia's mother had taught there too before moving to the West. Columbia University! It was very impressive. (Lore's mother stooped above the gasping lilies. She bent over the stuttering sewing machine.)

*Full disclosure*, Julia said: She and Asa had been lovers, on and off over the years. They'd lost their virginity to each other. They'd shared their first kiss in kindergarten! But that was all over now. A youthful dependency they'd grown out of. They'd been unhealthily close at times. (Their mothers had carried them side by side in their wombs. Their birthdays, a mere three weeks apart.) The last, disastrous time that they had been lovers was two years ago now; the depression they'd moved in then, the sense of staleness and being unable to make things right, proved that they were meant, for the long term, to be merely the best of friends. And Julia intended to find Asa the perfect match, the person *right* for him, she repeated. (She herself was in a dreamy romance with Simon, an up-and-comer at his design firm.) Had she mentioned that Asa was devilishly handsome and funny and smart? And a good, good, good person—he worked for the Environmental Defense Fund, saving the air and the oceans.

"The air and the oceans," repeated Lore. "That sounds like a lot." But Julia didn't smile. She was in earnest—Asa was some sort of saint.

Door after door: DO NOT ENTER: TEST IN PROGRESS. Lore wonders what precisely is going on behind these right now, what dark masses are being sought, what ugly secrets explored. Four closed doors in a row. Lore believes she can feel the humming of waves penetrating her skin, jostling and disrupting cells. It might not be good for the baby; she hurries on.

All right, all right, Lore said—she would meet Asa. (But she did not think a saint would be the right person for her at all.) For weeks she put off their get-together. She was in love with her new friend; this Asa was superfluous. But eventually she agreed to meet him at an inexpensive Greek place, his recommendation. She saw at once that he would expect to split the bill, and this pleased her. It suggested that he would not feel entitled to anything in particular. His physicality appealed to her: his disorderly curls and dark eyes and Roman nose, the broadness of his shoulders. He was three inches taller than she was, bearish and with a slow, delighted smile. He had the city quickness, its self-assertion, in his speech and in the movements of his hands. It was true that he wanted to save the air and the oceans, and he began to bore her somewhat with the details. There were so many dilemmas. We had to stop relying so much on foreign oil, and farmers upstate were struggling to get by, you couldn't begrudge them a chance to make an easier living—but the companies starting to buy drilling rights would eventually tear up the land and poison the waters. The Chinese needed to grow their economy, just as we in the West had had our turn, but their coal plants might be death to the chance to put a brake on global warming. Those were just examples of the big picture; now he got down to details: mercury and triclosan, lobbyists and building codes. He went on too long, in his worrying and his enthusiasm, and then he caught himself and turned the conversation to her. How many kids in her caseload? How do you teach a child to make the *sh* sound? She showed him, and he practiced in earnest as if he really were a six-year-old who had to do it from scratch, laughing at his own trouble. *A man*, she thought, not a cocksure boy. The few lovers she'd had were generally able to keep only one opinion in their minds at a time, and believed the definition of being a man was to make you hold that opinion, too. The city had a softening influence on men, Lore observed, without taking away their masculinity. Asa had a deep, hoarse voice that spoke of imperfection, of vulnerability. When he kissed her at her door, his hand, which lightly held her cheek, was tender, but he did not shift to conceal the tight pulse of his erection, and she gave over then; she chose: *Yes*.

Asa had his own version of the Story of Asa and Julia. Well, Julia, he said, a bit wearily. The longest, longest story. Always Julia had sent him away and called him back. She wanted no one else by her during the year after the rape. He must be near her all the time. And he—he owed her everything; he wished he had died rather than left her to walk that last half block to her apartment (the man had struck her in the head three times before dragging her into the corner of the crumbling Beaux Arts lobby, where she lay, disoriented, until a couple returning from after-theater drinks heard her moaning). There was so little he could do. He brought her gifts constantly—candy, books, flowers, funny little handmade cards announcing his love. He walked her to her therapy appointments, because she cried desperately before them, saying she didn't want to be made to talk about it anymore, but he, coached by her father, gentled her along, saying it would help her in the end. (In truth, he feared the therapist would drive a wedge between them, push Julia to blame him, awaken her rage.) They began, carefully, to make love again. Then Julia abruptly decided that she was going to Germany to study painting and this had to be goodbye; she might in fact never return. Six months later she was back and they took up where they'd left off—until Julia decided she preferred to be with a goateed fellow who worked in a bicycle repair shop in Brooklyn. It was like that always, at nineteen and twenty-one and twenty-four. Asa would leave docilely when she sent him away, come back when she wanted him again. Like a monk (an exaggeration: he had his affairs; but nearly, nearly) he went into retreat during the hiatuses. Just as she couldn't seem to fault him in any way for the rape, he couldn't seem to be angry with her for leaving. She was just—Julia. He loved her. He had always loved her.

"But not like *that* anymore, of course," he told Lore. When had this been? Four months after the Greek restaurant and the kiss at the door? Six? Perhaps it was not even a lie then. "Besides," he said, "now there's *you*—"

and he kissed her throat so gently that it sent tremors down her thighs and into her toes.

She did not in fact believe that he did not still want Julia *like that*. He was a man, after all. But she believed—she thought she saw, in his behavior toward her, and toward Julia when they were all together— that they had long ago put an end to it. His ardor left nothing to be desired. In bed he was frank and appreciative. It was hard at times to believe that he and Julia had ever been lovers at all. Julia was so fragile, so brittle even (when she was not well she did not eat much, and became quite thin and wan); how could robust Asa ever have made love to her without breaking her?

Asa said he understood now what adult love could be. Something where two people did not merge so completely that they had trouble figuring out where one ended and the other began, but rather the joining of two strong, separate beings, creating a future rather than trying, over and over, to redo the past.

"You're not afraid of us all continuing to be friends?" he asked, and Lore answered, Why should she be afraid? She adored Julia, and besides—so there!—she had been Julia's friend before she was his lover. If she had to choose, she teased, she might choose Julia over him. With whom did she go out more, to museums and to movies, for a good glass of wine (Asa was so cheap and so serious; he would rather spend the evening reading about hydroelectric dams)—with whom, to be blunt about it, did she laugh more? Julia, she told him. You better watch your step.

Lore halts and puts her hand against the wall. She has been moving too fast and has lost her breath. She had given Asa and Julia two months once she moved out. Julia would not be able to tolerate Asa's exclusive devotion, would start as always to chafe at his dependence on her. They would implode by the summer. But just before Thanksgiving, a friend saw them going into a movie on 23rd Street, clasping hands. Lore surprised herself, upon hearing this, by the melancholy she felt for them. What would become of them? Julia, with her dark moods, her terror of ever possessing what she wanted. Asa, with his longings for family life. Julia would never have children, she'd said it many times, and her therapists also advised against it. And now she, Lore, was the one who—though betrayed, though humiliated—would have a family, who had new life growing in her.

Whom did she miss more? Whom had she loved more, Asa or Julia? Or had she only been able to love them as a pair? "I've never really loved anyone," Julia said, one unusually warm early-spring day as they sat in Central Park. Lore was shocked. Julia held a bag of broken Saltines, which she was sprinkling before the pigeons. She said she'd lived in New York City for twenty-nine years and she'd never fed the pigeons. Ever since she was little and had seen the movie *Mary Poppins* she'd wanted to feed them, like the old bag lady on the steps of St. Paul's, but no one in this city ever did. Well, she was going to feed them now. She held the bag out to Lore so she could join in. The dark, plump bodies swarmed toward them, shoving and pecking at each other, uttering strident cries.

"People are right," Julia said. "They're disgusting." A pigeon climbed onto her sneaker and she flung it away. "Ugh!"

"You love Asa," Lore insisted. She was frightened. What did Julia mean, she didn't love anyone? Was she just having one of her days? Was this the first hint of a depression coming on? But Julia had seemed cheerful enough walking over to the park.

Julia turned to look at Lore seriously. "I don't know. I'm not sure I'm built for love."

"I don't know what that means," said Lore.

"That's why you're so great. You don't." Julia nudged at another pigeon to keep it from attacking her ankle. "Maybe," she said, staring at her skirt—it was striped, red and white, flared, Lore will never forget—"Maybe the closest I've ever come is with you."

Lore swallowed a sweet lump in her throat. She was quiet for several minutes and finally she and Julia got up and walked on toward Bethesda Terrace. The next time they spoke it was about a painting Julia was working on, a technical problem she was trying to solve involving the use of a deep purple and an external source of light (but Julia almost never showed even Lore or Asa her paintings, and rarely finished them; they never pleased her).

That evening something odd happened. Lore began to ask herself if she really loved Asa as she'd believed. If even Julia did not love him, had never loved him, could what she felt possibly count as love? She ran through scenes of their days together, probing what had been behind her actions, the things she'd said to him: had it been real feeling or just habit, had she ever been faking? After twenty-four hours of this she was convinced she was developing one of those obsessive thought disorders, and she put a firm stop to it with a big glass of wine and an evening planted in front of *Law & Order* and *CSI*.

About what Julia had said—about maybe loving her—she could not think at all, it pierced her too nearly, too beautifully.

Of course it had all been bullshit. Julia and Asa had been sleeping together for two years by then. Julia had stared down at her skirt because she didn't have the gall to look into Lore's eyes when she was lying. She'd said what she'd said—about Asa, and her feelings for Lore—to generate those obsessive, doubting thoughts, to destabilize what Lore and Asa had.

But Lore knows that is not really it, or not all of it. She believes—she will always believe—that Julia did love her, that she looked down into her lap out of shyness. It is not something she will ever be able to prove, to herself or anyone else, but she can feel again the warmth of Julia's skin in the spring sunlight, the naturalness of their bodies on the bench together, the way Julia looked at her when she spoke about love, calm and serious and troubled all at once. Julia meant what she said about Lore, at that moment. She meant it again at other times without saying it. Lore can feel the wind brushing her hair, the shrieking of the pigeons, the sweat of her feet in the heavy socks she'd put on that morning, the fresh and mossy smell reaching them from the lake. Oh, God!

A tug in a different place, starting right under the belly button, pulling down like a stuck trapdoor. Lore breathes deeper and walks quickly to the next Women's she sees, darts inside. She lowers herself onto the toilet, shifting briefly to center her weight, and reminding herself of Franckline's instructions. Breathe down into the belly. Let the voice out. But the pressure has already disappeared. Lore waits expectantly; a minute passes, then another. Where did the pain go? She curses. Pain for nothing, panic for nothing. She wipes herself, in case, and uses the metal bar on the right of the toilet to pull herself up. When was the last contraction? It seems like ages ago. Why all this waiting, when things are supposed to keep speeding up? She wants the speed, the pain, the progress. She ties her gown.

Without quite meaning to, she has roamed far. She washes her hands, pulls open the heavy door. She must go back, back to room 7. Franckline's face swims up before her. Come get me, Franckline, she thinks. Come find me. Come help me, come make it all easier. She sees herself leaning on the tall woman's shoulder, making her way with frail supported steps. Oh, come off it, she scolds herself. She is a strong, healthy woman of thirty-one, willful and able. (The image of leaning on Franckline was absurd: in it she was elderly, fragile, in no way herself.) She dislikes these daydreams of weakness that occasionally come to her. She used to imagine doing what Julia did: staying in bed for days on end, neglecting to eat or wash. Asa used the word "times"— Julia was having one of her times. He also said *depression*, and once in a while he floated *bipolar*. All this was terrible, of course—Julia suffered—yet it was a freedom allowed to her, Lore thought, to surrender so completely. The café where she waitressed paid her when she worked and let it go when she didn't, Julia's father sent checks to tide her over, and her friends brought soups and conversation. The therapist she saw twice a week (also paid for by her father) spoke with her, if she could not get out of bed, by phone.

During these periods Lore and Asa came over after work, bringing expensive sorbet or some other easy-to-eat treat—it was a worry, trying to get food into Julia. Clementines she enjoyed sometimes. They sat and talked to her, and Julia asked about their work and even laughed. You wouldn't know something was so very wrong except that she would eat so little and not get out of bed. Her father, who came to sit with her, went out when they arrived, to smoke a cigarette. Later he'd tell them that the minute they left she turned her face into the pillow and became mute for the rest of the evening. They were dreamlike, those hours in Julia's room. The lights were either dimmed very low or put up so bright they hurt Lore's eyes. This would go on for weeks or even longer, until one day Julia would emerge like a shaky chick, go to work again, paint in her studio, cook a little something for the meals the three of them shared in Asa and Lore's apartment.

Lore walks faster; she is not weak, is not slow. She is strong, able. Reaching the room where the man smiled at her, she peers in, but it is empty now, just a parking lot of steel and chrome. A nurse bustles by, carrying a large muffin on a paper plate—a whiff of chocolate, which normally would appeal to Lore but now makes her throat rise. Thoughts of Asa and Julia are like this smell—rich, intrusive, nauseating. In the middle term of her pregnancy Lore was nearly free from them. She felt expansive and fit, her mind full of strategy; any hated images were flimsy and fell from her easily. She was busy drawing up budgets and preparing applications for summer positions that would supplement her income. The sister of a friend at P.S. 30 ran a home day-care center that would take Soleil at three months, when Lore's maternity leave would expire. If finances became too difficult, she would abandon the city, return to Lockport or one of the smaller towns upstate, even—why not?—Hobbes Corners. She knew now that where she'd come from was just as good in many ways as here, and what had seemed to her so entrancing about the city, so desirable—museums, clubs, offbeat films, parks and plazas filled with remarkable-looking people—no longer interested her, or at least she would have no time for them. Surely that was what had happened to her mother also, dancer or no dancer: some illusion had faded, her essential not-belonging had been revealed, and the details that Lore, as a child, had thought of as so humble—the hems on her school skirts, a freshly baked potato for dinner—had revealed to her mother their essential decency and even beauty.

She is back at the picture of the seashore. Julia's voice rises up: *Someone taught this Thomas Eddington person that rocks look like this and the ocean looks like that and that it's especially arty if you make it a wee bit unrealistic with some pink dashes in the water and yellow on the rocks . . .*

*Enough*, Lore interrupts wearily. Again she spreads a hand on her belly. Defiantly, she celebrates the little flecks of humanity going about their business, the winsome sailboat, the melodramatically fading sun. She mentally deposits Thomas Eddington, 1993, in a large, disorderly room—a wooden shed on an old Vermont property, a cold wind coming in through the slats, the floor covered in drop cloths, meticulously dabbing on his colors of boats and sea, of sunbathers, of summer. He is pleased to be making summer during the winter. He is making summer as best he knows how. And that is honorable and fine, thinks Lore. (The nurse mysteriously changes direction, passes Lore again. That scent of chocolate: sludgy, sour.) It's a good picture after all, she decides. She doesn't care what Julia thinks, or Julia's mother, or the director of the fucking Metropolitan Museum. It has pleasant colors and evokes sensations of quiet, pleasant, lazy days. It reminds her—and strangely, memory slips in without a feeling of counterpressure, without distress—of summer days spent at the beach with Julia and Asa, or with Julia if Asa couldn't come, of the fierce heat against her face and the gulls trying to pick at the sandwiches they'd packed, and the cold waves bringing you back to life after you had baked yourself to a sweat. She was a poor swimmer, and Asa worked with her in the water, showing her how to coordinate her kicking and her breath. Julia called from the beach: "You can do it! Go! Go!" Lore was ashamed to be clumsy at something so rudimentary, something most children mastered by the time they were seven. But she slowly improved, and one Sunday Asa, in reward, bought her a boogie board and showed her how to use it. She swallowed salt water at first, and was slammed upside down on the beach more than once, but now she knew what to do when she went under and she didn't panic, just held her breath and waited for the world to right itself. Soon she got hooked on riding the waves, slick-feeling and fast under the board. Treading water and waiting for the biggest crests, jumping, feeling the triumph of having timed things just right, of being scooped up in the palm of the wave and enabled to fly. Next to her, on a different board, rode Asa or Julia, taking turns, allowing her to hog the new toy. Sometimes they shouted to her as they rode—"It's a good one!" or "Look at you, Supergirl!"—but Lore was too delighted to answer. Those seconds of speeding toward the shallows in a tunnel of rushing sound forged a solitude that was perfect and somehow sacred. At last she climbed with quivering legs onto the sand and threw herself back into her beach chair, spent. It seemed a great dream, to lie on the edge of a continent, looking out upon sundazzled, horizonless water. She expanded, stretched deep inside of herself, felt herself become pliable, capable of great acts of the heart. She might be more beautiful than she had imagined. She might be a heroine of some sort. She teased herself over these exaggerated notions but let them come and fill her with secret happiness.

Ahead, a burst of sound from an open room. A doctor—short, a little roundish, with dark hair, Indian perhaps, stands over a patient in a reclining chair, slightly smiling, but the patient, both of whose legs end at the knees, knees swaddled in thick white bandages, is laughing uproariously. And now mirth catches at the corners of the doctor's smile, and the smile breaks beneath it and the doctor begins to laugh, too, shoving his hands into the pockets of his white jacket, his body vibrating up and down. *Hoo-hoo!* the legless man laughs, a deep bass sound, and the doctor rumbles back *chuga chuga chuga!* his body trembling, and they go on trading their sounds back and forth, the doctor raising his right hand as if conducting the small orchestra they are making. The bubbles of this shared laughter enter Lore and make her shake a little too, smile and vibrate, as she passes, so that she conceals herself for a moment just past the door, trying to see in, trying to imbibe the effervescence a little longer.

As she comes in sight of the charge desk, Marina, the charge nurse, looks up at her grimly. "Ms. Tannenbaum!" she says loudly. "I've had two nurses looking for you. You are not allowed to . . ." Lore ignores her, entering room 7 and shutting the door. She stares out into the night pricked with street and car lights. Franckline arrives at the room a couple of minutes later, out of breath, her eyes reproachful. "I'm sorry," blurts Lore. How she hates that phrase! It's like trying to move sand around in her mouth. But she cannot bear Franckline looking at her like that.

"I needed . . ." She tries to explain, but falls silent. She doesn't know what she needed.

"What was I to think?" asks Franckline. "How was I to know where you were?"

"I didn't . . ." What didn't she? She didn't think. She had been angry. It seems like silliness now. Childish.

"I need to know that you are all right at all times."

Ah! Lore is ashamed! *That you are all right. At all times.* Lore has been uncooperative, ungrateful! Who else has made this offering to her—*that you are all right at all times*? Who else has taken this on as their duty? (She was tired. She was not thinking.)

She lets Franckline guide her onto the bed.

Back home, Franckline reflects, they might have said that a *lwa* had for a short while taken hold of Lore. There were girls and young men who disappeared for days or even weeks, and would be found wandering miles from their villages, hair matted with sticks and mud, dried blood on their thighs, talking of mad experiences they had had with eagles, vultures, crows. There was nothing to do but bathe them and try to understand the message the *lwa* intended. Bernard chided her when she told such tales. There are no spirits except the Holy Spirit, he said. He and his family had been converted by Protestant missionaries when he was fifteen. Franckline too believed in Our One Savior, and wore the cross to show it. But even here, 1,500 miles away from Ayiti, it was hard not to think that the spirits from her childhood occasionally entered other bodies and made themselves known.

When she'd come out into the empty labor room and had not found Lore in the hallways or in any of the bathrooms, she'd grown alarmed, thinking of those crow-plucked and eagle-harassed men and women, and also of the woman, a year ago last fall, too much methamphetamine still in her veins, who went up to the eleventh floor and out onto the roof and jumped. The woman had been delivered just a couple of hours earlier of a baby boy, and her nurse (Carmen Ingres, it was, poor Carmen) had left her resting, so she thought, with her boyfriend. When Carmen next poked her head in to check on things, the boyfriend was gone, disappeared into the dusk, and the woman had flung herself onto Sixth Avenue.

Franckline draws shut the curtains. At this hour, people across the way can see inside. "And we've got to put the monitoring belt on immediately," she announces, trying to smooth out the agitation in her voice. The girl nods, docilely, and Franckline feels as she affixes the stretchy straps that she is tying Lore to her, binding her to safety. She watches the printout for a moment, listens to the reassuring *lub-lub*. She is listening once again to the sound of her own child. Here is something else about a fetus at fifteen weeks: the bones are hardening and the ears are becoming intricately whorled. This child will look like any other child the world over, but it will be an American child and draw its first breath in American air. It will have the ways and sounds of this country in its life stream. Is this a good thing or a bad thing? It's true that many American children are spoiled. She sees this in the hospital: kids careening in the hallways, screaming and fussing, refusing to mind their parents. Not most of them, but some in a way that a Haitian parent would never tolerate. Or at least would never have tolerated back there. In their neighborhood in Flatbush, the children have a freedom and an arrogance that were utterly unknown to her and her siblings growing up. The American-borns sass their parents, whine about chores, expect spending money. The parents employ the same discipline they were raised with, but to reduced effect. The children are breathing American air and drinking American water; it cannot be helped. Franckline imagines all the things she will do for this child: mash up plantains for its breakfast, place a block near it and then far. Sing it songs in her unfortunately tuneless voice. Tickle its belly. She and Bernard are both lean but she hopes for a fat child, with squat, sturdy legs and busy hands.

All is well according to the monitor. Franckline glances at the girl, who stares down at her belly from her reclining position in the bed as if in disbelief that her child is ever going to dispatch itself from its swollen home.

A man pokes his head in, gray hair pulled back in a ponytail from his narrow, lined face. "May I come in?"

"Yes, yes!" says Franckline, and welcomes the man with a clasp of her hand. It's Jim, the orderly who works mainly in Gynecological Oncology but helps out in Maternity now and again, especially when a patient needs a ring or a bracelet removed. Franckline is glad it's him; he's always gentle with the women.

"It's really coming down, Franckline," Jim says. "Gonna be six inches by the time you head home. Maybe twelve inches by the morning."

"Is that what they're saying?"

"That's what they say. I'll take my grandkids sledding tomorrow if their mama lets me."

"Jim's going to take the ring off," Franckline explains to Lore. "Show him your hand, Lore."

Jim's figure moves toward her out of the bright light of the room, which feels smaller to Lore now with the view of the street shut out. "Oooh," he says. "Not too good. You've got to have this off, all right? I'm sorry. But when the nurses want something off, it has to come off." Franckline lowers the birthing bed and Jim guides Lore to sit on its edge, pushing aside the monitor leads. He takes Lore's palm in his and asks her to spread the fingers. She mustn't protest anymore, she thinks, she must be good, she owes Franckline for absconding and making trouble. (But she saw things on her travels. A painting of the ocean. A legless man laughing with deep delight.) From a plastic toolbox the orderly removes a rectangle with a silvery protrusion that looks like an oversized key. He slides this key under Lore's ring, explaining that it is to create a barrier between her skin and the cutting tool. He has to push to get it underneath. Lore winces. "I'm sorry, love," Jim says. He takes out something larger, a sort of rod with a small wheel attached to the bottom. He gives her his routine warning, saying that the blade can't cut her if she keeps still, there's the guard between her and the ring.

"Ready?" he asks, flipping on the battery.

Jim once told Franckline that it always made him sad to cut off women's rings; they always had some private meaning. Franckline concurs: the patients wouldn't leave them on all this time, right up through the hospital intake, if there weren't. Sometimes they are wedding rings, but more often, surprisingly, they are other types of rings entirely: flimsy gold bands with tiny gems that might have been handed down from some hardworking, immigrant grandmother, or cheap brass worn since the teen years. There are tears sometimes. The women hold up the damaged metal, peer disbelieving at what used to be a piece of jewelry, get anxious over what will happen to it next, ask for a bag, a box, a pouch, and fuss over where that bag or box or pouch will be placed. In some very particular pocket of their overnight bag, in their mother's purse. Jim proceeds very slowly, letting the wheel grind for eight or ten seconds, then shutting off the device. Every time he stops, he touches the growing cut with the tip of his surgical-gloved finger to let it cool enough for him to go on. Franckline has noticed that it calms the patient, too, to watch the cut coming little by little. The few minutes make a difference; she starts to absorb the loss. Who knows what may happen once that occurs? One of the stories Jim likes to tell is of running into a woman at the supermarket whose wedding band he had removed shortly before she gave birth. He didn't remember her, but she remembered him. "Once you did it I realized I no longer wanted to be married to the bastard. It's just Alice and me now. I'm much happier."

"About halfway there," Jim tells Lore.

There's no sound in the room except for the soft grating buzz of the cutter. Franckline strokes the band on her own finger. She will know to remove it long before it becomes a problem. That will likely not be until the third trimester. How beautiful that will be, knowing she's passed through the most dangerous period, and that with every week the child is more sound, more viable. She will set the ring in the cushioned box it came in, next to the empty one that held the crucifix she now wears.

Jim is getting close. He is a thoughtful man: he's worked the cut so that it extends a groove already in the pattern of the ring rather than slicing any which way. Sometimes the women balk as he is finishing up, and pull away—a dangerous thing. But Lore doesn't jerk or quiver; she watches the little wheel stoically, seemingly riveted by the tiny sparks it throws off, along with infinitesimal bits of silver. Franckline senses the enormous effort in her stillness. Jim pauses and gives Lore his routine warning, apologizing again, reminding her that she's perfectly safe if she keeps still. Franckline watches a slight jog, a little hesitation of the metal, and the cut becomes complete. Jim turns to his box to fetch a new tool, a tall, curved pair of prongs, and, fitting these under the separation he has made, he begins to stretch the two sides of the ring apart. Once there's a large enough gap, Franckline delicately removes it from Lore's hand.

"You were perfect," Jim says to Lore, who looks stunned. "It will start to feel painful as the blood comes back," he explains, putting his tools into his box. "But that's a good thing."

"Take care of this one, Franckline," he says, squeezing Lore's shoulder gently.

"I most definitely will."

"Where would you like me to put it?" asks Franck-line, when Jim is gone. She's got it in a baggie, is holding it up.

"It doesn't matter."

"I'll put it in this pocket here." Franckline unzips a little pouch at the side of Lore's duffel.

"Excuse me," Lore says. She gestures at the monitoring belt—can she remove it?—and Franckline comes to unfasten her.

Once the belt is removed, Lore walks into the bathroom, closes the door behind her, and drops herself onto the toilet. Tears spring up in her eyes, brim, then fall. All right, let them. She can still see the orderly's hand, broad-wristed like Asa's, and feel the painful pleasure of a man's fingers holding her own. The final give of the metal. She will never fix this ring. She could not bear to see the ugly seam in the once uninterrupted curve. *Everlasting love and life.* Maybe not. She reaches for the toilet paper, blots her eyelids and her cheeks. Ridiculous. But let them fall.

There is the trapdoor tug again. It's odd, how different this pain is from what has come before; perhaps the baby has moved down and is pressing more directly on the cervix. And then, so quickly that it tips her to one side of her seat, forcing her to put her palm against the wall to steady herself, Lore feels an urgent desire to push down, to push out the pain that is filling her up fast. Her belly goes liquid and she is nauseated; she is going to throw up. She calls out for Franckline, and instantly the nurse is there, kneeling on the floor in front of her, telling her, No, no, don't get off the toilet, ride it out here, lean against my shoulders if you need to. Lore leans into Franckline as if she were the pillows at the foot of the bed, wraps her arms hard around Franckline's frame. Franckline steadies herself with a hand on the toilet rim. "Let your voice out," she reminds Lore. "Bring it from way down." Their faces are inches apart and Lore can smell the subtle, spicy odor of Franckline's skin and something of mint on her breath. It diffuses the nausea a bit. She swallows. She doesn't want to shout or moan into Franckline's face, but the nurse is encouraging her, urging her, and she complies. She is sobbing, without knowing when she started, or how. The pressure inside her is tremendous; the baby pushes against her back, as if it wants to come out that way, and Lore too pushes without wanting to, fiercely, needing to relieve the pressure; something is looking for an exit; get it out, get it out, get it out!

But all that happens is that the contraction passes, leaving her with a reduced but still noticeable sensation of pressure, and her face bathed in tears and sweat. Franckline wets a towel and hands it to her silently. Lore draws it over her face with quivering hands. "A minute fifteen seconds," Franckline says. There is no smile or encouragement now; they're beyond that. Now they are in earnest.

Lore gets up slowly, sees that she's shat some small curls into the toilet. She is not embarrassed; she can't afford to use up her energy on any feeling as inessential as that. She flushes the toilet and swats at the seat with some toilet paper. "I felt like I needed to push," she says. "Is it okay to push?"

"I don't know. You ought to be fully dilated first. You didn't go through a clear transition."

"I feel like I want to push."

"It's possible, of course. We can't know unless you have another exam—or the baby comes out."

Lore's finger is throbbing, as the orderly has promised. The blood returns in thick, awkward pulses. At first she clutches it, to numb the hurt, but that proves worse. She has barely climbed back into bed, trying to avoid any pressure against the finger, when the next contraction arrives, and once again she has no time to do anything but lie back and draw up her legs and bear down with the frightful pressure. It is no baby pressing now but something else, alien and with damage on its mind. There is nothing proper to hold onto—not Franckline's shoulder or back, not the pillows, which are at the end of the bed; she can only grip her own knees, infuriated, ignoring Franckline's exhortations to draw in her breath and groan. Rebelliously, she screams, knowing that it will only waste her strength and rake her throat, knowing that screaming is for the weak and out of control, and that some other woman in another room will hear her and be frightened. When her breath comes back a bit she curses and bucks from side to side, protesting pain's fingerprints on her body. Franckline leans over her, instructing quietly, "Try to stay still," and Lore shouts, "I need it to come out I need to push," and Franckline says, "Push then," and Lore pushes, her feet trembling, her fingers (she no longer feels the damaged one) gouging into her knees. She strains with all her might until she genuinely expects to see a baby flop out on the sheet beneath her, until the pressure retreats enough to let her loosen her grip and lower her buttocks to the mattress.

Again Lore sponges herself with a towel Franckline brings from the sink. "Let's get you ready for the next one," Franckline says. She positions Lore over the pillows and phones the charge desk. "Patient in room 7 may be ready to push. Can someone call Dr. Elspeth-Chang?"

The next contraction comes quickly and lasts longer than a minute, but although the pain seizes Lore and shakes her, this time it does not panic her. The need to push has receded somewhat, and she praises Whomever or Whatever for this deliverance. No one told her that pushing might be so terrible, so rough-pawed and bestial, much worse than the cleaner, sharper pain of the contractions. The child is waiting a bit, has decided to stay with her a bit longer. In her birth plan, Lore gave orders that the baby should be laid on her chest as soon as it emerges and that she wishes to cut the umbilical cord herself. The idea of doing so in fact fills her with unease. The flesh, she imagines, will be tough and resistant under the scissors. She has a terrible image of not being strong enough to cut neatly, of having to twist and gouge to get the thing done. *I am father and mother both to this child.*

She turns her head, rests. Not long ago, Lore might have thought that any child of hers would have not one parent but three: her, Asa, and eccentric Aunt Julia. Julia, who didn't understand children, was afraid of them, and only once, that Lore knows of, ever painted a picture of one. A birth scene, in fact: a squatting woman and the emerging torso of a child. Unusual in that it stood in Julia's studio uncovered, unusual in that Julia did not speak of it bitterly, self-punishingly.

She seemed willing to appear almost fond of it. The woman had a flattened appearance and the background was luridly floral with the same harsh greens and reds and purples that Julia and Lore had gazed at in the Expressionist gallery that long-ago evening. The child's face was visible: a nightmare face, blurred and misshapen. Although Lore was afraid that any comment could spur Julia to throw a drop cloth over the easel and clam up, she could not resist saying that the child was awfully unattractive.

Julia shrugged.

"But I like it," Lore added honestly, meaning the painting. It captured something for her, something about her own mother, maybe—not what her mother might have gone through in labor so much as what she had gone through raising her on her own. Her mother had cared for her, but there must have been times when she'd felt she was being split open by the burden, that she was struggling to expel an ugly, indistinct scream.

"Do you? I'll give it to you."

Julia had never offered her a painting before. Never again would she. Yes, yes, she would take it, said Lore, thrilled.

Asa protested. He didn't like the painting, he confessed, and he returned to his argument about not having Julia's things in the apartment. Lore badgered him to give it a chance for a week or two. They tried hanging it in the living room, the bathroom, finally the bedroom. Asa held it to the wall yet another time. His eyes met Lore's, and then both of them broke out laughing, laughing so hard that Asa dropped the picture on the floor and Lore had to go get tissues for her eyes: there was no way that this painting could ever hang in their bedroom or for that matter anywhere else that belonged to them. It was simply too disturbing— too *Julia*. Without further discussion, Lore wrapped it in brown paper and stashed it in the hallway closet. When she moved out of the apartment, she spared it, left it resting neatly in its place against the closet wall. Even in her rage she could not damage one of Julia's paintings. Julia's soul resided in them; it would have been worse than a bodily murder.

Would Julia and Asa ever have a child themselves? Just weeks ago Lore would have called it impossible; Julia had neither the desire nor the stability. But nothing is truly impossible; every day makes Lore understand that more clearly. A child can travel down a three-centimeter-wide canal and emerge from an opening even smaller. Lore could one day decide to tell Asa the truth about Soleil, the truth he surely already knows. Not for his sake but for Soleil's. Although . . .

Franckline's voice rises up behind her. "You're leaking a little blood. I was watching to see if it would stop, but it's been going on for a few minutes. I'd like to get you onto your left side, okay? It improves the oxygen flow to the baby."

"Why? I mean, what could that be from?" asks Lore, her throat constricting.

"I don't know." Noises behind Lore, Franckline moving about.

"How much is a little? A little-little? Or more than that?"

"If it continues we're going to want to put an IV in," Franckline says, as she helps reposition Lore on the bed. Without asking, she is attaching the stretchy bands of the fetal monitor. Franckline's failure to answer Lore's question makes Lore's stomach go washy with anxiety. "Just to keep you hydrated," Franckline continues, "while we figure out what's going on. It could be broken blood vessels from the pushing. I'm going to get the doctor now."

Lore wriggles on her side to see if she can detect the blood, but her belly is in the way and she doesn't want to contort herself out of position. She's hot and a little faint. A psychological reaction, she tells herself: don't let your imagination get going. A contraction arrives, too soon, and there is nothing to do but grip the tight bedsheet under her fist. Her finger throbs again. She moans as best she can, surrendering almost gratefully to the pain that will for a minute or two keep her from thinking or worrying. She fights to stay still. Movement, she thinks, could increase the bleeding. In some unspoken prayer she wills the blood to slow.

The resident slips into the room, the same one from this morning, Dr. Merchant (she catches his draft of energy and a glimpse of his fine hair before she sees his face). "Ah, yes, the Department of Education lady," he says. "Sounds like a little excitement going on here. Let's take a look." He studies the paper that spits slowly from the monitor printer. Lore thinks he'll make some comment about it, but he doesn't.

He stretches on his gloves, then asks her to part her legs. He stops to lay a hand on her knee. "You must think we're all sadists," he says.

She clenches her teeth as he goes in—one more moment, one more moment, she repeats to herself, yet the doctor stays and stays. "Your water still hasn't broken," he says, and Lore feels vaguely reprimanded. The pressure of his fingers fills and then fractures every remaining private space, and she makes loud complaining cries that she knows will make no difference. "Seems normal," he says, pushing deep one more time, then withdraws. Lore turns her head into her arm, panting.

There is a heavy, wet trickling against her thighs. "Good news. You're at eight centimeters. One hundred percent effaced, zero station. You're going to have this baby this evening. I can't say what the bleeding is, but we'll be watching the monitor, and I'll come back in a few minutes. Franckline, start an IV, and let's get some oxygen ready, too." To Lore: "Don't do any more pushing, okay? You still have a little ways to go."

Lore begins to ask about the oxygen—is it really necessary? Will they stick a mask over her face? Must they go ahead with the IV? But she doesn't have time to say much, because she feels a new cramping, followed by a pain that doesn't start somewhere like a quiet bass line, but is at its loud, crashing climax almost immediately. She hears herself yelling out. Something seizes inside, and her belly goes hard as rock. Her inner vision dims. Something falls on the floor with a ping, strangely audible amid her own cries (she hears herself as an echo rebounding from some distant, craggy surface). Hands move around her, gripping her shoulder, asking what is hurting, what is wrong? She does not know! She does not know! Oh, God, it does not stop! Her belly is stone. Someone struggles to hold her down.

"It's okay, it's okay," Franckline says to Lore, who realizes in that moment that it's not okay, that something very bad must be happening. She can't figure out if sound is still coming out of her mouth. Hear me, hear me, please! Things start to happen very quickly: an unfamiliar voice, Dr. Merchant giving orders, a wad of something is pressed to her groin. Her bed detaches from its place, rolls out the door and down the hallway. Footsteps beating alongside. She is aware of a rhythmic pumping between her legs, like the glug-glug of shampoo coming thickly out of a bottle, and then a gush. People are calling out. She can't catch her breath and she thrashes on the moving bed, but Franckline—she is sure it's Franckline—holds one arm firmly and asks her to stay calm, the calmer she can be the better, they need to get her baby out. She'd like to be still but she can't; the pain is in charge, filling her eyes with sparks.

The lights grow brighter and then dimmer again. People talking in some sort of gibberish. Fear, terrible fear, crashes in, worse than the pain, so that she yanks a mental curtain down against it in haste. *I am not afraid.* The light grows brighter than ever, the rolling bed halts abruptly, and Lore would not have believed that there was room inside to feel any more suffering, but now there is an agonizing intrusion, so intimate and so objectionable that her lungs burn with the screams she emits.

The body is not a solid thing but a sac of liquids netted with tendons and bones, of wriggling, dividing cells and traveling electrical pulses. It is prone to leakages and eruptions. It rocks on the tides of hormones. In the early weeks of Lore's pregnancy, a group of cells divided off from the embryo and became the placenta, branched with blood vessels like a great flat leaf. Some error—neuronal or in the genetic coding or due to a harsh bump against the corner of a school desk, who knows—resulted, at thirty-two weeks, in a small piece of the placenta pulling away from the uterine wall. Lore never knew of it; the blood that leaked out was trapped between the rest of the placenta and the wall and did not flow down. As the child grew closer to being born, the placenta sheared away further, but the new blood too continued to be concealed, held in by the great amniotic sac. When Lore's labor became advanced and the baby descended sufficiently in the vaginal canal, some of the trapped blood trickled out of her body. And when Dr. Merchant punctured the sac—it would have been punctured, spontaneously or intentionally, sooner or later—the large pool of blood was suddenly released, and the uterus clenched in a great and pauseless contraction.

Who can be blamed for this? The mother felt no symptoms. The labor nurse checked her and her baby's vitals frequently. Dr. Elspeth-Chang ordered the routine number of ultrasounds—and ultrasounds do not always detect even advanced abruptions. Dr. Merchant followed the protocol of breaking the membranes of a woman whose advanced labor is progressing erratically.

What if there is no one at all to blame?

Lore's veins are dehydrated, hard to locate. Franckline palpates for anything puny, slippery, rolling. She plunges in once and misses. No time left for error. She brings her attention to a fine point, locates a line, and goes in. "Let's move," says Dr. Merchant, and Franckline hooks up the bag of saline while running alongside the bed.

A young woman wearing a bed jacket, taking a break from the boredom of her labor room, flattens herself against the wall, alarmed, eyes dropping from the shrieking patient to the blood spattering onto the floor.

No scrubbing, just move it, and the catheter has to go in *now*, calls out Dr. Mankowitz, the attending, as they wheel into the ER. Lore's screams when the catheter pierces the urethra will join the collection that appears in Franckline's dreams sometimes, along with the ragged woman's shouts of "Father!" at the cathedral in Port-au-Prince, and the silent spasms of the child who never actually cried, never made one sound of life.

Lore is rigid and fighting as they lift her onto the surgical table. She is powerful in her terror and her rage. The tech tears open Lore's gown and the quick dump of Betadine turns her belly into a spreading or-ange-yellow stain. The oxygen mask is wrestled over Lore's mouth and soon she is mercifully absent. *We are coming*, Franckline says silently to the baby within.

Dr. Mankowitz tells the anesthesiologist to intubate.

The tech calls out that the baby's heart rate has plunged to 45 beats a minute. *We are coming*, repeats Franckline, to Lore this time. She and the tech put grounding pads under Lore's thighs and tip her gen-tly into position, a pillow under her right side. *That's right, you don't even know we're here. Sleep, sleep.*

"Cut her vertically," Dr. Mankowitz tells Dr. Mer-chant. The scalpel goes through the subcutaneous flesh and the fascia and into the peritoneal cavity. How quickly a body can be cut, how easily its innards ex-posed. Now the uterus. Franckline applies clamps to keep the walls open. The cavity is a sea of blood. She fights a tickle of nausea. Down beneath this blood is a creature, alive or dead, just as inside herself there is this same flesh, fat, fascia, blood, creature. She suctions while the tech sponges. Willfully she narrows her mind to the suction tube, the cavity dimensions, the rapid controlled movement of her tool. Her ears filter out all extraneous noise.

"That's as good as we're going to get," says Dr. Mankowitz, and Dr. Merchant sloshes into the uterus like someone dropping his hands into a small, extremely dirty sink.

In a moment he has extracted the bluish rag of flesh, its eye sockets filled with blood and its ears tiny teacups of blood, blood thickly painted all along the torso and legs, but they can see that it is a girl. The tech suctions mucus out of the nose and mouth and the child shudders slightly. Imperceptibly, they all lean in: the child is alive; there is time and there is hope. Dr. Mankowitz cuts the great fleshy rope and the child is handed over to a NICU nurse, to be carried to the warmer and hooked up to an IV.

Dr. Merchant pulls out a ragged chunk of placenta.

"Zero, one, zero, zero, one," calls out the NICU nurse.

The blood is still coming from Lore's belly and from between her legs, soaking the sterile drapes, forcing Franckline to stop suctioning for a moment and replace the grounding pads. The uterus is not contracting, says Dr. Merchant.

"Where's that A positive?" Dr. Mankowitz demands.

Franckline checks the monitor. Lore's heart rate is rapid, 160 beats a minute, and her blood pressure is low. The uterus looks big and boggy, like a collapsed balloon. Dr. Mankowitz calls for Pitocin and Methergin. Suction, suction.

"I can't wait. Get me some fucking O negative," Dr. Mankowitz tells the circulating nurse.

"Good, good," says Dr. Merchant, talking to himself, as Franckline suctions. He is removing smaller pieces of the placenta from the uterus, like a potter quickly but carefully scraping smooth the inside of a clay bowl. The blood transfusion begins. A breeze of expectation lifts up the little crowd—the thick red nourishment will work its magic. But Lore's blood pressure still drops, and drops again. Franckline looks up and sees, like a shadow drawing away from a window, the soul retreat from Lore's face. Oh, Jesus Christ my Savior, she thinks. Oh, Papa Ghede, save her. She hardly hears as the anesthesiologist calls out a Code Blue. She returns to her suctioning; she must think of nothing else. Beside her, focusing on his task too, Dr. Merchant scrapes.

Marina, pulled in for this purpose, is setting up the defibrillator, pressing the pads to Lore's chest. One shock. Two. The line on the monitor jumps and then settles like a spent wave. Head down, suction, suction. A sizzle of pain in Franckline's left ovary. Mapiangue and Papa Ghede, no. Protect the child.

"One, two, one, one, one," calls out the NICU nurse. Franckline hears a tiny mewl. Or did she imagine? Do not think, suction, suction. In another few moments she is aware of the warming bed trundling past, the opening and shutting of the operating theater's doors. The NICU voices disappear.

"Keep going," Dr. Mankowitz tells Marina.

"She's clean," says Dr. Merchant.

"In fifteen seconds I'm going for a hysterectomy," says Dr. Mankowitz. The heart pulse can be heard again, a bit stronger, but still thready, quick.

"Doctor, I think the bleeding is slowing. Give it another thirty seconds?"—Dr. Merchant. He is massaging the uterus with his hands to encourage it to draw up.

"The A positive is here," says the circulating nurse, who is ignored.

Then—they all feel it, the absence of something, an abrupt quiet—Lore's heart stops beating. Heads swivel to the monitor. "Keep going," says Dr. Mankowitz again to Marina.

Again she shocks the girl. And again. The second time, Lore's shoulders shudder and she gurgles as if trying to dislodge the tube in her throat. Her blood pressure reading ticks up: 55 over 30. *Come back*, calls Franckline.

"She's passing a little urine," says the anesthesiologist.

"Again," says Dr. Mankowitz. With the next defibrillation they hear the heartbeat, though it is rapid, hounded. For long minutes they continue their work and wait. The hiss of the siphon, the squelch of the saturated sponges hitting the bucket. The irregular beeping of the machines. Franckline can see the uterus finally begin to pull closed like a drawstring purse. Dr. Merchant's hands, continuing to massage, are steady, but she feels the tense heat rolling off of him.

Blood pressure 80 over 50. Heart 85 beats per minute. Thank you. Thank you, Papa Ghede. Thank you, Jesus Christ our Savior. Hold off death. Deny death. Death must not exist today. Blood pressure 90 over 60. Heart 75 beats per minute. Lore's face goes from gray to pale; she is inhabited again.

"Okay," Dr. Mankowitz finally says, straightening. "Sew her up." The pace in the room slows. They have time to be careful now. Dr. Merchant dips and tugs with the surgical thread, creating neat dashes: twenty, twenty-five, thirty. There is no hurry. Gradually, Lore's insides are returned to her privacy.

Moments later the anesthesiologist removes the breathing tube, and Franckline and the tech begin the process of cleaning Lore up. Patiently they wipe her with warm water and antibacterial pads, dry her. The bloody sponges sit in a tub, waiting to be counted, and the canister of Lore's blood mixed with amniotic fluid will be measured, too, so that they will know exactly what came out of Lore's body as well as what went in, what she lost to have this baby.

Franckline, the anesthesiologist, the tech, the circulating nurse, and the two doctors stand by to see Lore come around. Her breathing is steady if a bit rapid. After a few minutes, her eyes open. They are bright and unfocused, and she appears to be seeing something that isn't a blood-spattered group of olive-gowned hospital personnel.

"Soleil," she says.

They gather in a room near the back nurses' station, telling each other what has just happened, going through the minutes one by one. At 5:34 PM, the incision was made. At 5:39, Dr. Mankowitz requested a transfusion of O negative. The circulating nurse, Alicia, takes the record. Dr. Mankowitz questions Franckline about the course of Lore's labor: her pains, her blood pressure, anything else that would have signaled a concealed abruption. Franckline answers as calmly as she can, shows him her log. Would he point out something she had missed, something she has done wrong? But he hands the log back to her, apparently satisfied. When he and Dr. Merchant and Marina depart, Alicia turns to Franckline. "She was *gone*," Alicia says. "Sixty, eighty seconds. Gone."

Franckline nods silently. She is extremely tired. They—Franckline and Marina and Alicia and the tech and the two doctors, and the machines that do their bidding—they grabbed a woman held in Death's grasp and shook and shook and forced Death to drop her. And now they are very tired. Something aches deep inside her loins. She can no longer tell if it is fatigue or something distinct from that.

By the time she changes her scrubs and updates her notes, it's past seven, past the end of her shift. Tomorrow morning she'll be back again. She should stop by Lore's post-op room and check in, make sure the new nurse is up on everything. But there are a couple of things Franckline needs to do first. At the charge desk, signing herself out, she greets Billie and Cynthia, two nurses who have just come on and have heard all the evening's news from Marina. There is a woman in room 9 who is going into transition, and Billie heads over to tend to her.

Once again, Franckline walks to the far bathroom, casting a glance at room 7 as she passes. The bed has been stripped and remade, fresh pillows laid out. Lore's duffel is gone, presumably transferred to post-op, and the floor is still damp from mopping. In the bathroom, she shuts herself into a stall for a quick check. No blood. She puts her hands over her face and lets the shaking come on. She is sorry, so sorry—for what, she cannot say, only that things should have come out differently.

Cold streams through her body and she hugs herself, teeth chattering, unable to stem the tight, jerky movements of her legs and head and arms. It was a test, she thinks, and she has failed. A sign. Her baby is in trouble and will be born, like Lore's, blood-drenched and gray.

*Franckline.* She hears Bernard telling her to be reasonable, to understand, as the Americans do, that the world is full of chance, that not every event speaks with meaning. One out of every hundred pregnancies—that is not Bernard talking; it is she herself who knows the figure—one out of every hundred pregnancies results in an abruption, a quarter of those very serious, so that a nurse who has practiced for several years will most certainly come across such cases now and again.

*Yes, Bernard,* Franckline agrees.

*And was not the baby caught up in the hands of those who cleaned it and warmed it? Did it not survive?*

*Yes.*

She takes her time in the stall, letting the shaking slowly diminish, and when she feels ready, she splashes herself with warm water and leaves for the third floor. There, outside the NICU, she scrubs and dons surgical gloves. When she opens the heavy door she has to refocus for a minute to find the babies, so tiny are they and so overwhelmed by the masses of boxes and screens and consoles and lights and cords. The room—they call it the Big Room; babies who are moving toward discharge are transferred to one of the smaller ones beyond—is completely interior: there is no way to tell whether it's day or night. Or, rather, perhaps, it is always night here, despite or because of the bright fluorescents everywhere. It is quieter than usual, except for the sound of the ventilators and oscillators and the intermittent beeping of the monitor alarms. Franckline doesn't come here often; she stays carefully, as much as possible, on the side of birth that manifests in lusty cries, in pink health. The NICU babies trouble and prick her, sending her back to old memories and empty questions. (What might all of these machines and medicines have done for her tiny nameless boy? Might he be a strapping child of thirteen today, attending school, running with strong legs in the streets, bending over a plate of *sos pwa*?) Besides, it is better to allow the family and the professionals to draw tight their circle of healing; she cannot be helpful here. But tonight she cannot stop herself. She must see and know. She asks for Baby Tannenbaum, and is waved over to a nurse named Barbara, with whom she is acquainted.

"Ah," is all Franckline can say, looking down into Baby Tannenbaum's warming bed with its low, see-through sides. There is another occupied warming bed next to her, but the rest of the row is empty, which makes it a slow week. Like many of the other babies, Baby Tannenbaum is wearing only a diaper and a cotton hat, and has EKG and heart sensors attached to her chest, with another sensor on her abdomen to keep track of her temperature. There's an IV in one hand and another in a foot, in addition to the umbilical IV, but the thing that truly unsettles Franckline, despite her experience, is the ventilator taped against the child's mouth all the way to the ears, obscuring her expression. The intubated babies always seem to Franckline like beings that are still living in some subterranean universe, smears of life waiting to emerge.

Compared with the child next to her, a two-pounder, Baby T looks like a pro wrestler. But what's going on inside that brain of hers—what damage might be unspooling, or, more hopefully, healing—no one knows. Not the neonatologists, not the nurses, no one. Only time will reveal that.

"You're taking a special interest, eh?" Barbara asks in patois. Barbara is from Martinique, and their languages are close enough that the two of them can understand each other. It's a welcoming, intimate sound, like an offering to a guest, and it soothes some deep homesick urge in Franckline, even though she hears her home language every day in the neighborhood where she lives. It's different, erupting here, in the middle of Manhattan, after a long working day. Yes, the language gives her that pang.

"*Ma wi*—I am," says Franckline. "She had a bad time, the mother. There's no father in the picture, nobody."

"Mmmh," says Barbara, a grunt of disapproval— not of Lore, but of a fate that offers a woman on her own a damaged child.

"What do they say?" asks Franckline, meaning the neonatologist and the respiratory therapist.

This is not something she is supposed to ask, and Franckline knows that Barbara is forbidden from giving out such information. But there is no one here just now to observe their communication, and Barbara will understand that Franckline's need to hear is pressing. She'll know that she can trust Franckline to let it go no further. Barbara says, quietly and quickly: "She lost a great deal of blood, but her lungs are strong and she should be off the ventilator by tomorrow. We're still waiting on most of the labs. She'll have a brain scan in the morning."

Franckline reaches down and places two large fingers on Baby T's bare right side, which is less encumbered by cords. Barbara looks away, pretending to check a monitor. Baby T startles at the touch, her foot kicking up. A good sign. Her flesh is warm and very, very new. Franckline feels the rise and fall of her ventilator-controlled breath. A new creature has been deposited into life. And

Franckline's gift has held: she has lost no baby, no woman, since coming to this lucky land. Baby T kicks out her foot again, looking as if she wants to protest Franckline's intrusion, scrunching up her eyes as if she might cry. But of course she can't cry with the tube in her mouth, and it's another child who begins to bawl right at this moment, the thin, insistent cry of the extremely young. Franckline turns to the sound, and as she does, it strikes her that she has touched Lore's baby before Lore herself has done so. She feels a sting of remorse.

The other baby continues to cry, thinly, fiercely.

"Ah, the loud twin," says Barbara, indicating the child with her head. Franckline walks over and excuses herself to a male nurse, who allows her to view a set of twins in his care, names posted on their isolettes: Michael and Mickey. To do so she has to pass a little girl named Flower whose IV is stuck directly into her bald scalp, making her look in fact as if she has just been plucked with her stalk intact. The twins are dark-haired, and each weighs in the vicinity of four pounds. The loud twin appears to be Mickey. "Oh, shush," says the nurse good-naturedly, expertly weaving his hands through Mickey's leads and IVs to put the child over his shoulder and pat his back. "Always bitching about something."

"Handsome, aren't they?" he asks Franckline. "This is the bad one. So I hold him close to my heart."

"But you have to pay attention to the good one, too," Franckline scolds, smiling.

"I do, I do. But I love the bad ones the best."

"Michael and Mickey?" Barbara says, when Franckline returns. "They've been here for three weeks. No one has come to see them. Not once."

And now an alarm sounds, a rapid beeping that rises above Mickey's wails. Barbara looks up calmly, confirming that it comes from a machine in another bay, and another nurse moves unhurriedly to adjust a lead. The NICU seems to be stirring for the new shift. A mother and father arrive to visit their child. The neonatologist on duty begins his rounds a few minutes later, along with his resident and the cardiologist and the respiratory therapist. It's time for Franckline to go. She spends a quiet minute gazing at Baby T, trying to fix all the details in her memory: the color of her skin, the shape of her head, the way her ID bracelet hangs on her tiny wrist. There must be something too vivid in her own eyes, because when she takes her leave, Barbara gives her an appraising look. *Don't get attached,* she's warning. *Don't let it matter too much one way or the other.*

On the way to post-op, Franckline checks her watch. Bernard will be putting dinner on the table soon, expecting her.

Glenda, a younger nurse, greets Franckline at Lore's bedside. "She's hanging in," Glenda says. "She has a fever, but her vitals are pretty good. She's on a Dilaudid drip."

Franckline pulls up a chair. She takes Lore's hot hand and holds it in her own, pressing it gently. Lore's hair splays in damp sections against her pillow. Her skin is pale and her eyes move rapidly under the lids.

"Dr. Elspeth-Chang was just here, and a woman named Diana is on her way over," says the nurse. "She's Ms. Tannenbaum's health proxy. Someone who works with her, I think."

"May I?" Franckline asks the nurse. She goes to the door for Lore's chart. She holds the folder on her knee and removes Lore's birth plan.

IN THE EVENT THAT THE BABY DIES, I seek the following:

- *to be able to see and hold the baby for as long as I wish*
- *not to be given tranquilizers or drugs that blunt feeling*
- *to arrange the funeral myself*

She turns back one page:

IN THE EVENT THAT THE BABY IS ILL OR
HANDICAPPED, I seek the following:

- *I would like all procedures and any medications given to the baby to be explained to me.*
- *I would like to touch, hold, and breastfeed the baby if possible, and as often as possible.*
- *If my baby has a severe handicap, I would like a full discussion with the pediatrician before any treatment is embarked upon, so that I can explore all of the options.*

Franckline moves back to the bed and again takes Lore's hand. The nurse moves discreetly to the corner of the room, folds a stack of towels.

The sedated and the comatose hear what one says to them.

"Have they told you about your child, Lore?" Franckline asks. She leans in very close. "It's a girl. She's doing all right. She's in the intensive care unit, and she's breathing and her lungs are strong. Her skin is a beautiful pink, and she has the prettiest little ears. She should be off the ventilator by tomorrow. They are going to test her brain, Lore, to see if everything is all right. I know you've thought of everything. I know that you will know how to take care of this child no matter what. So, you must get strong again, fight off this fever, so that you can hold the baby in your arms and give it what it needs. The hospital will know what to do until then. Be easy, Lore. Be easy." Lore's head moves restlessly from side to side on her pillow, indicating either that she hears Franckline or else that the sounds of speech are disturbing her slumber.

At the charge desk in Maternity, Franckline speaks in low tones to Marina. Will Marina help her—again? Marina, sympathetic but hesitant, replies that there's only Dr. Merchant right now; the others are occupied. "Someone else, please," says Franckline. Not Dr. Merchant, no, not just after watching him loose a river of Lore's blood, not after standing next to him as he moved and cut amid Lore's organs. Marina peers at her assignment chart more closely. Dr. Phillips just signed out and went to change; perhaps she will be willing. Marina walks off in search of the doctor, who returns a few minutes later, looking drawn and annoyed, but gestures for Franckline to follow her into a small room down the hall. She smooths fresh paper over an examining table, and as Franckline shucks her elastic-waisted scrub pants and lies down, she becomes someone else: not a worker, not a caretaker, but another body to be opened up and peered inside of. *Relax*, she tells herself, as she has told so many others. The doctor squirts warm gel over Franckline's belly and pushes it around with the ultrasound wand. She watches the screen, stubbornly silent, making neither upbeat nor worried sounds, stops, clicks to take a few images, then pushes the wand around some more. More wanding—does the child, Franckline wonders, somersault playfully away? Does it feel disruption, distress? Does its heart still beat at all? Finally the doctor tells Franckline to slide down and put her feet in the stirrups. "Sorry," she says briskly, as she guides the probe inside. Click-click on the console.

Withdrawing the probe, Dr. Phillips announces that Franckline looks just fine; the baby is a normal size, the amniotic sac is normal, the heart is normal. The bifurcation in the uterus does not seem to be having any effect on the fetus's development (she points to the uterus's left-hand chamber). She hands Franckline a towel with which to wipe herself off. "I don't see any reasons for concern here. I can't tell you what the pains are. Might just be stress, Franckline."

"Thank you, Doctor."

"Take your time. Close the door behind you when you go."

Franckline wipes and wipes until she feels dry, then pulls up her pants, fishes for the key to the locker that contains her street clothes. So things are all right for another day, another two days. Tonight, with Bernard, she will decide—again—whether to speak the news.

Lore walks down corridors searching for her child's room. Left, right, left, right: the doors are open but there are no babies here, just grown men and women turning in their sleep, or being comforted by their families, or calling out for help. She can't help them, not right now, her child needs her, her Soleil. At the end of a corridor, after many rooms, a stout woman in a police uniform waits expectantly to hear Lore's business. Lore tries to explain but her tongue will not make any *L*'s or *R*'s, any *S*'s or *Th*'s. She tries to enact the exercises she knows so well. Click the tongue ten times just behind the top teeth. Relax the lips. But the *L* will not sound. The *R* will not come. *R* is the most difficult sound of all. Children rarely master it before age seven. She places the sides of her tongue between her back molars and presses against her upper teeth. A hissing silence.

"I am here!" cries Lore to the policewoman. "I am here!" But she cannot explain what she is here *for*. She pushes the tip of her tongue between her front teeth. She holds a tongue depressor crosswise between her lips. She sucks on a great straw. *S* is *S* as in *Sock*. *Sh* is *Sh* as in *Shoe*.

The drugs toss her, float her on dreams of paralysis. She is trussed up in ropes. She spins in a black atmosphere. She sees Soleil, bound in strong nylon wires to a white crib: she must rescue her. Soleil! Soleil! Lore's lips move rapidly, she calls out, and the nurse by her side pats her hand and strokes her arm until she settles again. Even sunk as she is, she grasps at the notion that there is some *outside* to the universe in which she now tumbles, that she must struggle up and pierce the shroud to meet it. She sinks back down, into darker dreams of horned shadows passing along a wall, of a heartbeat loud enough to rock her trapped body like a rowboat in a squall.

The nurse strokes her arm, adjusts the Dilaudid drip, notes in the log Lore Tannenbaum's pulse.

Down the hall two doctors eat dinner in the conference room. Dr. Lee: a vegetable soup and chicken stir-fry made by his wife, also a doctor. Dr. Glendinning: supermarket lasagna. They often take their dinner together, methodical eaters who like having a companion to whom they need not speak. For hours they have torn flesh open and sealed it up again; they have inflicted pain and quieted it; they have upheld life and prolonged dying. They are gods at the feast after the Games, but instead of the homage of slaughtered and fragrantly roasted animals, here is ground beef layered between ribbons of precooked semolina; instead of great bowls of wine, there is Dr. Lee's astringent green tea. There are no crowds, no toasts, no dances stepped to their honor. They ask for so much less—a few moments of quiet, a small heap of calories to enable them to continue. They do not need to figure in the songs of poets.

Dr. Glendinning gets up to find some salt. Dr. Lee pours the remains of his warm tea down the sink.

The day's weary are leaving—on subways, in cabs, by foot—and the fresh healers are coming in. The nurses arrive at their charge desks, orderlies check in with supervisors. Natalie Komlosky, age two, is curled up asleep at the bottom of her mother's bed, having briefly met her new baby brother and been told her mother cannot hold her because of her stitches. She dreams of strawberries and a basket of soft leaves, and of a pink ball she lost last week that now rolls to her from a hidden corner. In the morning she will know: no matter what losses are visited upon us in the waking day, our nights will always comfort and recompense us. Natalie will always love the night now: its inventions, its richness, its sympathy. There are creatures of the day (alert, energetic, strict, practiced in loss) and there are creatures of the night (rebellious, vague, imaginative, greedy), and Natalie moves to join the night creatures, receives their hot, loyal embrace.

Arthur Niccoli, seventy-seven, dozes in his bed. They took out the tumor in his right lung, the size of a walnut; a very clean operation, the surgeon said. Arthur supposes it is good to be still alive; he supposes it is worth it even though Maria is gone, her gentle snoring next to him in bed, the swell of her ample hip. She would have been seventy-five this May. She is gone and so is the past they had together. How he once ran up steep streets simply to feel his body pitch against the wind; how strong his hands were with a hammer or spade. Great too was the alchemy of children, the making and shaping of them, watching them grow tall and free. He supposes there remain, still, sunlight across the carpet in the morning and the comfort of good socks at night when you are reading about Churchill or Khrushchev (reading about Churchill in bed is no small pleasure), and the grandchildren who remind you of what it was like once, when you had sap and the world seemed to tumble out of the sky anew each morning. He slides an eye over to George, sprawled in an armchair, his long legs halfway to the bed. His son is frowning at his laptop and pecking at the keys. He might be writing an office memo or he might be playing one of those crazy games even the grown-ups waste their time on now. Arthur Niccoli smoked for fifty-two of

his seventy-seven years; surely in a couple more the
doctors will have to go inside him again, and it will
be worse next time, the growths elongated and bound
more tightly to the organs. At first he'd refused even
this operation. Let the tumor take its chances with
me, he said. But George and Mimi had coaxed and
begged, how they coaxed and begged! It was enough
to make you wish you were dying all the time, to see
how much your children wanted to keep you around.
I did it for you, he thinks wearily, you selfish children, you grandchildren. I did it for you, Dr. Can-
berra, so as not to injure your pride. He recalls the
woman he saw this morning as he was wheeled to
surgery: a great madonna in blue scrubs, her hand on
her enormous belly. She'd wandered with her nurse
into Pulmonary like a visitation from another planet.
Why, he'd wondered as the young nurse pushed his
wheelchair by—why keep me, when what I am passing now is the real thing, the true event: this swollen
belly with the hand powerless to hold the great force
in. In a matter of hours someone new would be alive
in the world. When he was coming out of sedation,
Arthur saw the blue-scrubs madonna again. Her belly
was split open to reveal a spinning globe. There were
dark blue seas and green lands. He thought: I will be
gone soon, but she will carry things on for me. Why

can't they understand, the children and grandchildren and the doctors, that she will carry things on for me?

Dr. Merchant, on a double shift tonight, examines a new admit to the ward. His hands tremble as he pulls on his gloves. Why shouldn't they? The flesh is weak and the mind troubled until one has seen much more of disaster and death. Dr. Mankowitz asked him a number of questions. What had occurred just before the hemorrhage? How deeply did he probe when he broke the patient's water? As Dr. Mankowitz took down his answers, Dr. Merchant could see that the older man judged the thing to have been inevitable, that he pursued his points merely for the sake of the weekly meeting in which the surgeons and residents would review the problem cases, the near-misses and the disasters. Dr. Mankowitz will have to speak to what happened with Lore Tannenbaum, and Dr. Merchant may also be asked to respond. But if Dr. Mankowitz doesn't fault him, if he does not fault himself, why does he feel such dread? He puts two fingers inside the woman on the table, as gently as possible. It is terrible to be here inside another woman. It is somehow not right. He should have gone for a cup of coffee. He should be home watching television with his wife. Adrenaline churns, propping him upright, making his fingers and hands crackle with painful electricity.

("Four centimeters," he tells the patient.) There are eleven hours and twenty minutes until the morning.

A man in shirtsleeves chants softly by his laboring wife, who takes his hand and lets the vaguely familiar music wash over her. It is not lucky to have a baby on Shabbat, her husband once told her, then apologized, saying it was an old superstition, nothing to dwell on, but it stuck in her head and now that the sun has gone down on this Friday night, she cannot forget it. She was not raised religiously but her husband was, in another life. Now he prays, knowing that the God he normally does not believe in will forgive him for this appeal that is driven by fear and a strange nostalgia. He petitions God for the safe passage of his son into the world, for his wife's suffering to be brief. But mostly, as he was taught long ago, he prays to praise God, designer of the universe, giver of life and will and knowledge of the right. Do not ask for too much from this God, who is beyond our petty pleadings and who knows what role he has designed us to play in his Creation. *Mi chamocha, ba'elim, Adonai—Who is like You, Lord, among the gods that are worshipped? Who is like You, glorious in holiness, awesome in splendor, working wonders?*

And Lore murmurs in her half sleep, the Dilaudid bringing her pictures, atmospheres. Diana approaches Lore with a bowl of fruit, saying that they called her and of course she came in right away. The fruit is for Soleil, she says. Soleil must be hungry. She will go to Soleil and feed her right now. Bring me! Lore calls. Unhook me! But Diana disappears down the hall, trailing a wash of dirty water behind her.

Lore wades into the water, going deeper and deeper, and now she is swimming far out into the waves. A foam board, like the board Asa taught her to ride on, tumbles by, and she tries to catch it, to hold onto it, but misses. She snatches at another board—no. A wave flips her under the water. Asa reaches out his hand and pulls her onto his chest as he back-kicks toward the shore. He is solid and unafraid; he will keep her head above water. She was never a good swimmer, but he made her a better one.

Ach! cries an orderly, disgusted at the water covering the hospital hallway. Messes, always messes. Nothing but messes in this place. A pigsty. A slaughterhouse. And no one thinks to clean anything up. It all falls to me. He gets out his mop of white tails, his sprays and suds and sponges and cloths. The blood is coming up through the tiles, and no matter how quickly he mops it up, it seeps back more copiously. *Faster*, Lore urges. *Hurry.*

Waiting in the corridor are Asa and Julia, nodding at her from a distance. *We didn't mean for there to be so much blood*, they say. *We had no idea.* Their voices grow thin on the wind. And Lore replies with her eyes: *But how did you not expect blood?*

Then Franckline is talking to her, slowly and clearly, saying the baby is in some sort of special place, that her lungs are strong and that she is waiting for Lore. They must test the child, they must torment her, but one day they will let Lore come and soothe her and hold her. This is real, Lore thinks. Franckline is in the world: solid, permanent. Lore tosses between the waters and this still bed. She tries to wake and listen. For as long as Franckline sits by her Lore will know what is real and what is not. *I am coming*, says Lore, but her arms are tied down and her tongue will not create the words. *I am coming*, she says all the same, sure she will get there, knowing she need do nothing more than wake up from this dream and she will be able to hold her Soleil.

*Wake up, wake up*, she whispers to herself, but she cannot yet quite wake.

# ACKNOWLEDGMENTS

My heartfelt gratitude once again to my agent, Anna Stein, and my editor, Tony Perez of Tin House Books, both of whom pushed this book to become the best it could be. Also to Anna's assistant, Alex Hoyt, and to Nanci McCloskey, Diane Chonette, Jakob Vala, and all the Tin House folks who continue to make the process of publishing such a pleasure.

Thanks to the large number of people who spent their time to ensure that my portrait of a hospital labor would be accurate; any errors are my own. These helpers include Jan Kaminsky, RN, Ilena Kasdan, RN, Laurie Konowitz, MD, Jennifer Lublin, MD, Einat Manor, MD, Johanna McCarty, RN, Laura Ratner, Pamela Schachter, Claudia Taubman, MD, JoAnn

Yates, CNM, and above all the extraordinary Tracy Claxton, RN. Rabbi Hannah Orden aided me with my inquiries about Jewish prayer. Thank you to Reverend Rose-Marie Dominique, who patiently answered my questions about Voudon, and Professor Elizabeth McAlister, who referred me to her. Thank you to Tara Lissade for general knowledge about Haiti, and to Enrique Urueta for his preternatural sleuthing skills. Thank you to Jonathan Ratner for his rigorous spousal copy editing.

Thank you to Margot Livesey, Randall Kenan, and Paula Whyman for invaluable feedback, and to my irreplaceable writers' group—Joanne Fisher, Therese Eiben, Lynn Schmeidler, and Philip Moustakis—for nursing *Eleven Hours* along.

Thank you to the many members of Mothers & More—too many to name individually—who helped me with various labor-related questions, some of them ridiculous.

Profound thanks, as always, to my nearest and dearest, Jonathan, Abraham, and Hannah, who support and encourage me and keep me on the right track in the ways that count.

PAMELA ERENS's second novel, *The Virgins*, was a *New York Times Book Review* Editor's Choice and was named a Best Book of 2013 by *The New Yorker, The New Republic, Library Journal,* and *Salon.* The novel was a finalist for the John Gardner Book Award for the best book of fiction published in 2013. Pamela's debut novel, *The Understory,* was a finalist for the *Los Angeles Times* Book Prize and the William Saroyan International Prize for Writing. Her essays, articles, and reviews have appeared in publications such as *Elle, Vogue, The New York Times, Los Angeles Review of Books, Virginia Quarterly Review,* and *The Millions.*